W9-CBT-257

A
DANGEROUS
LIAISON

A
DANGEROUS
LIAISON

Jocelyn Davey

Walker and Company
New York

Copyright © 1988 by Chaim Raphael

First published in the United States of America in 1988 by the
Walker Publishing Company, Inc.

Library of Congress Cataloging-in-Publication Data

Davey, Jocelyn.
    A dangerous liaison.

    I. Title.
PR6035.A64D36   1988   823'.914   87-18990
ISBN 0-8027-5689-1

Printed in the United States of America

10 9 8 7 6 5 4 3 2 1

THE MARQUISE DE MERTEUIL TO THE
VICOMTE DE VALMONT
*"You will serve Love and Revenge . . . The hope of
vengeance soothes my soul . . ."*
Paris: 4 August 17—

THE VICOMTE DE VALMONT TO THE
MARQUISE DE MERTEUIL
"Conquest is our destiny: we must follow it . . ."
Chateau de—: August 17—
—Choderlos de Laclos: Les Liaisons Dangereuses

1

PART OF VICKIE'S attraction was that one wanted to know what lay beneath that quiet self-contained surface. Some women generate this feeling. In *Madame Bovary*, the moment Emma comes on the scene one wonders if one should be ready to expect that something very surprising is going to build up around her. In the early pages she is just Emma Rouault, a farmer's daughter; but one feels it nonetheless, and all the more strongly, of course, when one begins to know about her dream-life in the convent.

There was something in Vickie that stirred the same kind of question. People who met her never saw her simply as Victoria McKenzie, a bright girl from Oxford who had written a prize-winning book. The clues to what lay beyond this were not immediately obvious. To say that she looked rather plain didn't take one very far. Ambrose Usher had picked on something else, again with a clue to *Bovary*. "She is very pale, isn't she?" he had said to Laurence. "But not negative—very positive, piercing." Having started a thought, he bubbled on in his usual way: "Like Emma, you know. You remember what Boulanger says about her: 'She has eyes that pierce one's heart like a gimlet.' And he loves her being so pale. He says he adores pale women. I do, too. And *you* do, which is rather more important."

Laurence hadn't said anything. One took things from Ambrose without too much complaint. Even when there were problems, Ambrose was allowed to look in, with friendship the only involvement. Laurence was about to break with Vickie, and Ambrose knew it. Why haven't you told her? he was really saying.

Once the book had her famous, one was encouraged to dig deeper from hints that it gave. There was violence in the book that she had expressed in her own way. She had written of a powerful man of action, but quietly, calmly, as if reining in her own passion. One could have known that when murder threatened in her own world she would have a response ready to deal with it.

What is it that turns a scholarly chronicle, full of academic research, into a paradigm of one's own life? Somehow or other she had come to terms, in the book, with the evil that lies in ambition and ruthlessness. She was to discover the reality of this in person, and hated it. Yet as a historian she had identified with the passions that enveloped her central character. If it had never surfaced as affection, the human sympathy had been very strong. It was this that had made it such a good book.

None of this was explicit on the sunny late April morning on which she stood by the kitchen table in her flat, mainly one hugh book-lined room with a view of Westminster Abbey in the distance, stirring a Bloody Mary and waiting for the one o'clock news. The Bloody Mary was to let a decision work itself to the surface. She had been offered a very interesting and lucrative writing job, and would have to consider the proposal in more detail that evening at dinner. In many ways she was tempted to say yes, though vaguely suspicious of the man who had made the offer, one of those barons of industry one knew very little about. She did have an alternative, the offer of a lectureship at Bristol University. Maybe she could combine the two, though the writing commission sounded as if it would be very full-time. The truth was that she seemed to have lost the

2

power of decision. She was carrying on with her work, functioning normally, everyone thought; but behind everything, governing everything, was the emptiness in her life now that Laurence had gone. She felt dead, longing for revival. If Ambrose had been around she would have turned to him. But he was away, lecturing in America somewhere. In any case, she had to take the decision herself. It was just that Ambrose was so easy to talk to.

She had switched on the radio and was stirring her drink absentmindedly. As she heard the first words of the news summary, the hand raising the glass for a first sip stopped dead in air. People one knew didn't figure in a sensational news item, especially if one was due to dine with them that night. Yet there it was. A letter-bomb sent to Lord Cranford's office at the publishing house of Aston and Wren had been detected and defused by a member of his staff.

In the news itself, there were a few more details. The police refused to say that it was the Irish at work, but admitted the bomb was similar in design to those that had been used during the recent IRA campaign in London. The man who had discovered the bomb and defused it was Lord Cranford's personal assistant, a man called Felix Morgan. To the public at large, Lord Cranford was always thought of as head of the hugh business known as UEI—United Engineering International, but the report explained that he had bought the old publishing firm Aston and Wren some months earlier, and enjoyed it as a diversion from engineering. Aston's had published a book attacking the IRA, so the motive for the bomb seemed clear. They must have discovered that he often went in to Aston's early in the morning to go through a few things, as chairman, before driving to the vast UEI skyscraper on the Embankment. Presumably they

3

thought that security would be slacker at Aston's, which was why they had sent the bomb there.

Vickie knew about the publishing background, but it still seemed odd to hear it trotted out on her radio. A bomb at Aston's! She thought of their warren of offices behind Covent Garden. They would all have fallen into dust with even a puff of explosive, as buildings like that had done in the blitz. Obviously they were right about the anti-IRA book *Evil in the North*. It had been written by an Irishman—Something Fitzgerald—who knew his stuff and had been ruthless on some of the IRA leaders. Ruthless not in denouncing their policies but in exposing their hypocrisy and corruption; how half the money collected in America was salted away by them in Swiss bank accounts. Names had been given, but no libel action pursued. She remembered hearing of an interview that Lord Cranford had given—the reporters would be digging it out soon—in which he had told a journalist that as chairman he could vouch for the accuracy of all books published by Aston and Wren. He expected the same thoroughness to be applied to the books as to his UEI products. To the IRA he must have seem personally responsible. In effect, he had sent himself a bomb. It was ridiculous, but very plausible, perhaps, to an outsider.

She had put the Bloody Mary down during the news, listening carefully for anything that might surface in the wind-up. Now, with the news over, she picked it up and as she took her first sip, the phone rang.

"Is that Victoria McKenzie? This is Felix Morgan, in Lord Cranford's office. Have you heard what happened?"

"Yes, I just heard about it on the news. Is all okay?"

"Absolutely. That's why I'm ringing. Lord Cranford thought you might wonder . . ."

"About dinner tonight? Yes, I did."

"No change," Morgan said. "You know the boss. Doesn't bother about unimportant things like a bomb."

"Was the BBC story right? How did you know how to defuse it? It said something about your war service in Vietnam. I gathered when we met that you were American."

"My Yankee accent gave me away. Yes, it was Vietnam. It was a specialty of mine there, and this one was easy. A piece of cake—isn't that how you English put it?"

She had only met him once, when Cranford had first summoned her to Aston's to listen to his proposal, and on that occasion, too, when she sat waiting in the outer office and Morgan had talked to her, there'd been a bit of the same "you English" attitude. It had irritated her; clearly a ploy of some kind. Perhaps he was pushed into it by the atmosphere of Aston's, almost a parody of Dickensian higgledy-piggledy, obviously a strong contrast to the American slickness he was probably used to. He would enjoy exaggerating his distance from all this precisely because he himself looked and sounded almost English, or New Englandish: tall, fair, and quite pleasantly mid-Atlantic in speech.

She didn't mind it so much this time. Some of her normal reserve, icy and inhibiting very often, melted a little when she thought of his having the courage to defuse a bomb.

"Weren't the police annoyed with you for tackling the bomb yourself?" she asked.

He laughed. "They *were!* Can you beat it? They said it could have confused the evidence. I offered to reassemble it for them, good as new. They were a bit nervous."

It was a nice thought. Vickie smiled. "It *is* the IRA, I suppose," she said. "Because of that book. Have they had a lot of trouble about it?"

"A great deal, it seems. I got this from Josephine Trout, one of the directors. There's a preface which thanks her very warmly for her work as editor and indeed stimulator. She says that she has had a lot of threatening letters. The police asked her if she could spot any likenesses to her letters in the way the address of the bomb was set out—handwritten. She couldn't, of course."

"A bit hard on Lord Cranford," Vickie murmured. "Why didn't they go for the author—Fitzgerald, isn't it?"

"It seems that young Mr. Fitzgerald is a little too wily. Trout says he's been invisible since the book came out. In any case, the boss is a better target if they want publicity; his connections with the government and all that. Still, it will be good material for you when you do the book."

"*If* I do the book," Vickie said. "I haven't made up my mind yet." She paused for a moment, breaking off deliberately from the rather jokey give-and-take that had developed and that was not her style. But in beating a retreat, she was led into a practical question that *did* concern her. "Can you tell me if anyone else has been told about my possibly doing the book?" she asked. "I hate gossip, especially before it has a real foundation. I suppose Lady Cranford knows."

"I wouldn't be sure," Morgan said. "She won't be there tonight. She's away in Scotland. She's an actress, I suppose you know, and she's doing a play that's having a four-day run at a little theatre in Glasgow. I imagine that the boss *has* told her, but you never know with him. He's probably not told anyone at Aston's yet. He likes to keep things to himself."

"I suppose he might have told Warren Faversham," Vickie said.

"Oh, that's right," Morgan agreed. "It was Faversham

who put him on to *Man Alive*. He felt that the boss would like it, and he did. Raved about it.''

Man Alive, a biography of Paul Kruger, the Boer statesman, was the book that had made her famous. The Oxford University Press had published it, and it had won a number of prizes. She was always a bit apprehensive now, hearing it praised. Could she ever have a success like that again? She'd had to work on it for four years and the memory of that time brought back a lot of things, good and bad.

"Yes," she murmured. "He told me that Faversham had given him my name. I suppose he *may* have told him what he had in mind. Well, it doesn't really matter. Thank you for ringing. Seven-thirty, I think he said.''

She was about to put the receiver down, but Morgan seemed to want to go on. Typically American; they never stopped. She hated long telephone conversations, unless it was part of a personal friendship. With outsiders, the telephone was just for information. If one wasn't on guard, it became a permanent intrusion. There was no way of avoiding having a phone in London, but she had very firmly resisted installing one in her tiny cottage in Kent. There was a call-box in the village, and that was quite enough. She had never really missed it when Laurence was in her life and she had been immured in the cottage writing *Man Alive*. It had been enough to go to the call-box outside the post office at a set hour to see if he would phone.

Morgan was droning on about how much he'd enjoyed *Man Alive*, what a success it had been in America, all the translations . . . but her mind had switched back to Laurence. No phone calls ringing now in the village call-box at eleven o'clock, when he would leave his wife watching TV while he took the dog out for his night walk. There was something exciting—she had to admit it—in the secrecy. Did spies feel it in the same way: one call-box speaking to another, deep calling unto deep?

She missed it, but she missed so many things. The book for Cranford would absorb her, but not personally, the way *Man Alive* had. That was why she was hesitating. It would just be a job. There would be all the papers to go through, the evocation of the big business scene, the allies, the enemies. But would there be a nodal point of excitement? She was increasingly aware of how much she had needed this. Everything about Kruger in *Man Alive* had thrilled her, once she was involved. This was how writing worked. One had to wake up every morning, eager to push forward, wondering what event, what idea, what phrase would take over. With *Man Alive* it had never failed. Kruger had become part of her, or she of him. She was *inside* him. Perhaps this instinctive feeling could only happen with someone who was dead, whereas with Cranford . . .

"Yes, I would like to," she heard herself saying. She had been making polite noises while Morgan talked, and now he had asked her if she wouldn't have lunch one day. There were things about *Man Alive* that he wanted to ask her. "But that's just an excuse," he said. "I hate having lunch alone. I suffer through not being an Englishman going off to his club. Besides—shall I admit it? I like female company."

"When you're not defusing bombs," Vickie said, and the thought of the bomb again broke down her reserve a little. "Won't you be there this evening? The BBC report gave one the impression that you never let Lord Cranford out of your sight, and vice versa."

"Oh, no. He wants you all to himself tonight. You'll probably see a side of him that he never shows to me. Of course, I'll wheedle you into telling me all about it when we have lunch. You *will* come one day?"

"Yes, I should like to." They left the date open.

Warren Faversham, chief editorial director of Aston and Wren, was sitting at a corner table at Brooks's Club with his old friend, the writer Giles Corby, who had just got back from a lecture tour in America built around his superb picture-book on English country houses. They had known each other at Cambridge in the late 1930s. Both were unmarried, and had many tastes in common. At lunch normally, they might have pursued these delicate links of old friendship, but today the talk was inevitably of the bomb story, which Corby had spotted on the club's tape machine.

"What do you know about this chap Felix Morgan who defused the bomb?" he asked Faversham.

"Ghastly man," Faversham said. "He's been around everywhere, all over the office, since Cranford took over. Gets in at the crack of dawn and takes Cranford's post before the staff arrives. That's how he discovered the bomb in time."

"He's American, isn't he?"

"Oh, I don't hold that against him," Faversham said indulgently. "Live and let live, and all that. It's the way he operates with Cranford, not exactly toadying—in fact he's quite bright, rather amusing. But he just fixes everything for Cranford, the boss, he calls him, to make sure he doesn't miss a trick. You feel he's got everything under his thumb."

"How do you get on with Cranford himself? I met him once or twice a few years ago at parties when he was just plain Herbert Thomson. Seemed harmless enough."

"Our little Herbie. Well, he may have been all right then, before the publishing bug took him. The man's gone mad about publishing. We thought we could take the money he's put in because he'd just be a technical chairman, but he's into everything. The bomb serves him right, really. That statement he made about *Evil in the North*. He made it sound as if he'd written the book himself. No wonder they put his name on the bomb. The real person to blame, if they'd only known, was the Trout, our dear Josephine. She edited it and was desperately keen. It isn't a bad book, but one doesn't have to be blown up for a book, even a good one. The author's got more sense: Elliott Fitzgerald. He's taken himself off to Saudi Arabia to write a book on the Arabs for some enormous fee. I suppose when the Arabs get too hot for him he'll go off to write a book about the Israelis. Very sensible man. Never runs out of subjects, and always keeps out of trouble. Now let's see what we'll have."

The waiter had come up. They immersed themselves in the menu for a few minutes, and then the wine-waiter appeared for a more important discussion. The room had filled up. The English were at lunch in their clubs, snatching a few hours of vestigial opulence while the pressures of history pushed England down and down. At Brooks's, one was still floating comfortably—at least till about three o'clock.

They were starting with a few oysters and a bottle from M. Arrigeaux's special stock of Chablis with which he kept the club supplied. "What a joy it is to get back," Corby said. "I like their clams and all that, but—" He waved his hand around happily. "It still goes on. What a relief it is."

"Didn't they treat you well there? I suppose you were on the go with TV and all that."

Corby smiled. "It was fun when I got to San Francisco. There's plenty of good fun in New York, all our old pals, but on the coast it's a new life: no holds barred. A very enveloping experience, you might say. A bit awkward, though, when I was on the Johnny Carson chat-show. I'd been billed as working for British Intelligence during the war, and it was all about how well did you know Sir Anthony Blunt. Very awkward."

"Hallo, Giles." A tall man with a wizened face had

stopped at their table. "You've been raking in the dollars in the U.S.A., haven't you, with your book? I'm surprised the CIA let you out. Don't you agree, Warren?"

They talked banteringly for a few minutes, and the man went off. "Not such a joke," Corby said. "It was strange when I went through Immigration this time. I had a strong feeling that they were particularly interested."

"Oh, they always look one up in the black book."

"No, this was different. I've got on to one of their lists, somehow, and it's no fun. Once they take this line, it's forever, I believe. I expect they know whom I'm lunching with today, so they start looking at *you,* and then *you're* on the list. Maybe it's the other way round. Perhaps they *started* with you. . . . What about this fellow Morgan, chasing round your office at the crack of dawn, looking through all your files. Do you think he's a CIA type?"

"You mean dirty-tricks department? He certainly knows about bombs."

"*Was* it by the IRA?" Corby asked. "Did the police say?"

"Oh, you know the police. They never say. Certainly looked like it. But you know—I had a sudden idea about it when we heard the news. Suppose it *is* the IRA, okay. But what a marvellous cover it is now for someone who might want to bump off little Herbie. It would be like having a perfect alibi. Lord Cranford found with a bullet through his noggin, and everybody would be sure it was the IRA. Like to have a go?"

"If only I had a motive. But what about at Aston's? Do you have someone in mind there?"

Faversham took a sip of his Chablis with great delight. The idea was going nicely, and it had been a sheer improvisation. "Of course I have someone in mind. I bet she's at home now cleaning a revolver."

"She?"

"Certainly. Surely you've met our Emilia. If Aston's was a Western, she'd be playing the sheriff. Very handy with her .38 Colt."

"Of course I've met Emilia. She's certainly tough enough. But what's her motive?"

"Her *motive?* Isn't it obvious? To get her ancient rights. She's seething at Cranford having taken over, and Emilia St. John Marritt in her white blouse and tie doesn't take something like that lying down. She's very choosy at what she takes lying down. Among other things, it has to be feminine."

"Ha, ha. But why should *she* be so concerned? You're *all* seething, aren't you?"

"Of course we are. But it's special with her. Her mother was a Wren."

"A WREN? Women's navy? What's that got to do with it?"

"Oh, you idiot. Not a WREN. A *Wren:* Aston and Wren. Granddaughter of the original William Wren. Emilia's determined to get it back into the family one day. And now, if she plays her cards properly . . ."

"Very nice," Corby said approvingly. "Hercule Poirot would like the idea."

"I don't think I've convinced you," Faversham said sadly. "But you'll see, you'll see."

Later, when they said goodbye, a thought crossed his mind. Odd that Giles had found U.S. Immigration inquisitive in a new way. One would never be surprised now at things slipping out. George Sekelis had rung him from a call-box in Suffolk a few days before to say that a man in a pub there was asking him all kinds of questions. Of course, people in pubs always did. Still . . .

Emilia St. John Marritt was herself lunching at a club less than a quarter mile away from Brooks's, with pretty little Rhodine Tonbridge as her guest. When the Reform,

12

after years-long agonies of doubt, had finally, in 1981, become the first major old-style club to open its doors to female membership, she had nipped in quickly to get herself nominated and elected. It was one way of getting even at last with the cruel fate that had deprived her of enjoying the title that would have come her way from Grandfather Wren automatically if only women had equal rights. Her mother's father Wren had been awarded a baronetcy in 1920 for his outstanding position as a publisher—perhaps also for large contributions to the Liberal Party. Her own father had died when she was very young, and she had been brought up, in effect, by Grandfather Wren, whom she had adored. Sir William Wren, Bart., self-made, and more Gladstone than Lloyd George in his stern puritan ways, had passed on to her his clearly established set of values—discipline, cold baths, family pride, national honour. She was an only child, and would have inherited the title if only the English laws allowed title to pass equally through the female line. With or without the title, he was her grandfather, as proud as he had been over Aston and Wren, and increasingly bitter at the fate that had befallen her.

She had started at the bottom in the firm under Grandfather's eagle eye, shortly before his death. The Astons had long since faded out, but the Wren strain was weakening too. She had become good at the job and concentrated, when her state in the firm took her to the level of director, on the financial side. But publishing firms go up and down, and this was a time when this once great house, so famed for its legendary heritage of Victorian and Edwardian authors, was clearly losing out with the younger generation of writers, and living more and more off its backlist. American publishers were besieging them with offers of takeover, but though they needed the cash, most of the directors, and especially Emilia, stood firm against this. If the ship had to sink, let the Red Ensign

13

be at the mast. It was different when Lord Cranford came into the picture as a major investor. He was as English as could be, and would clearly be giving them the cash they needed on a patriotic basis, the way people went on lining up to buy *The Times*. At this stage, Emilia was his strongest supporter, partly because she thought there were echoes in him of Grandfather Wren. Behind Lord Cranford, she saw a straightforward Englishman, Herbert Thomson, who, like Grandfather, was entirely self-made. As everyone knew, he had started off sweeping the floor in a Yorkshire metal workshop. What had happened in the next stage was not so well known. How he had risen from five shillings a week to become the chairman of a huge combine like United Engineering International? One didn't ask questions. It was enough that now, as Lord Cranford, with time and money to spare, he was willing to save a famous English publishing house from being swallowed up by foreigners. In the interviews with the directors, he had been totally benign, showing no sign of a plan to run everything himself, with ruthless changes as he saw fit. That had only emerged later, and it was ironic that the man through whom he sent down his instructions—this Morgan man—was himself a foreigner, an American, however polite he seemed in his personal contacts.

But there was a way, now, of getting rid of Cranford and getting Grandfather's company back. She positively purred with delight when she thought how this had happened—and so quickly. She could hardly wait to tell Rhodine that it really seemed all clear now. A month earlier, when she had told her about the possibility, it seemed too good to come true, and it wasn't easy to keep her informed while Rhodine was travelling, first in Tokyo and then in Singapore, for the advertising company she worked for. It was only three days ago that the final confirmation had emerged about the huge sum of money Emilia would be getting to make it all possible. Rhodine had got back only the night before, and they had fixed up the lunch. Emilia had said that the sum was beyond all her dreams. She wouldn't say more. "I'll tell you at lunch. It's incredible, they can't refuse. I'll have the votes. That monster will have to go. Wait till you hear."

They had become friends only recently. Rhodine Tonbridge, very successful in advertising, was soft and feminine in the way she dressed and spoke, the very opposite in style to Emilia. She was of medium height, with softly waved fair hair, wide blue eyes, and a complexion of peaches and cream, a throwback, almost, to a flapper-type in looks, despite the tough job she held in the business world. She had been very hesitant when Emilia had suggested that she too should join the Reform Club to help build up a nucleus of women members. "Oh, I don't know," she had said in her gentle, half-cockney speech, looking round the male-dominated crowd of lunchtime drinkers filling the vast patio open to the distant roof. "I don't see myself among all those bowler hats."

"*What* bowler hats?" Emilia asked with Grandfather's literalness.

"Oh, they're all invisible, but don't you see them? Bowler hats and umbrellas, every man-jack of them. I hope you'll go on inviting me to lunch here—it's so funny—but I'm better off normally in purple slacks at the Dog and Duck."

"It's you who are being conventional," Emilia said affectionately. "Your advertising lot could do with a few old-fashioned standards instead of finding a new fashion every week."

"Yes, I know. I think I'm just reacting against my name. My parents so admired Cecil Rhodes and all those male Anglo-Saxon virtues that I have to keep saying no to everything that brings it back. Still, it's nice here, in a daft sort of way. *You* like it, anyhow. It suits you."

It did indeed suit Emilia, with her tall, lean look, black skirt, white blouse, and narrow pale blue tie. She was happy with Rhodine teasing her this way, and certainly a quiet table at one end of the vast luncheon room—the Coffee Room, as it was called—was a splendid place for a talk. Grandfather had been a member, of course. The food was no longer as distinguished as when the renowned Alexis Soyer was chef, the greatest in London; but his lamb cutlets à la Reform could still be ordered, and for those with a taste for wine—not Emilia, as it happened—the cellar had some carefully racked treasures.

They had gone straight in, but before Emilia could launch her news there was, of course, the bomb. Someone in Rhodine's office had heard about it on the BBC and told her. "Did you see it?" she asked Emilia. "I've never seen a bomb. How big was it?"

"No, I didn't see it. The police took it away. But I spoke to the Inspector, Detective Inspector Green—seemed to me very intelligent for a policeman. He told me that it was quite a small packet, came through the letter-box."

"How clever of that man to discover that it was a bomb, before it went off, I mean. How did he know about bombs?"

"Not all that difficult," Emilia said briskly. "Quite easy if you're used to a gun mechanism and know some electrics. But yes, it was good that he did it all, defused it and all that. He's American, you know, and was in the U.S. Army in Vietnam. Apparently he was a bomb expert there. In fact I think he was rather a whiz at electronics generally."

"Would it have blown the whole place up?" Rhodine

asked. "You would have hated that, all the old buildings there."

Emilia seemed almost to go pale at the thought. "I couldn't bear it if something happened to the first floor, Grandfather's old room. They would never be able to rebuild it. Probably knock everything down and build a skyscraper. But I don't think it was big enough to blow up the building. It would probably just have disposed of Lord Cranford."

"You wouldn't have minded that, would you?" Rhodine said, looking up from the menu folder that the waitress had now brought to the table. "Solved all your problems."

"Oh, no need for that now," Emilia said firmly. "Wait till I tell you what has happened. Let's order, and then we can talk. It takes hours for the food to come."

Their table, at the eastern end of the room, offered a view of the Reform at its best, the huge Coffee Room festooned with brass fittings and glittering chandeliers. Down one side near them, tables were laden with endless varieties of smoked fish, ducks, turkeys, and hams in corpulent magnificence, salads, pickles, and desserts. Smoke rose faintly from the dishes settled on hot plates. It was food in Victorian amplitude, the participants still almost entirely male—with their invisible bowler-hats—as far as the eye could see.

The waitress took the order-chit that Emilia had filled out, covering the plainest of fare, with haddock at its centre, and the wine-waiter, hovering nearby, was told to bring a jug of cold water. He disappeared, leaving behind a palpable whiff of distaste. Emilia leaned over the table to her friend. She touched Rhodine's hand gently, her eyes sparkling.

"You'll never believe it," she said. "I couldn't keep pace with it—all in three weeks. But now it's official.

17

I've become rich. I can buy him out. Everyone should have an uncle."

"You mean the art collection comes to you as well?"

"It's all to be included. Enormously valuable. Everyone always said so, but I never believed it. Of course I never had any idea that I'd inherit anything, especially the collection."

"But how did it happen? You weren't at all clear about it before I went off. You thought there might well be other members of the family over there, and there was the museum . . ."

"All cleared up," Emilia said happily. "No members of the family in the running. He was unmarried, and he and my father were only children, as I am."

"But still you didn't expect . . ."

"Not at all. Never. He was absolutely remote. My mother always said that there was something very odd about him, as if he was slightly dotty. But he'd made a fortune in oil and sold out years ago to one of the huge oil companies—didn't Rockefeller start there?—and just concentrated on buying pictures. He'd run away from school and gone to America without anything in prospect. But he struck oil on a bit of waste land he had, and it gave him a fortune."

"He never helped your mother at all after your father died?"

"No. He and father had had some terrible quarrel and they never made it up. He knew that Grandfather Wren helped Mother: we weren't all that short. So all we got from him was an occasional Christmas card."

"Didn't you want to see him, or at least the collection?"

"I did try once. I wrote to him a year ago, when I was going to New York, to ask if I could see him, and his secretary wrote back to say that he'd be in Mexico or somewhere. When I was in New York I heard that he

18

was unmarried and a complete recluse and that he'd promised all the pictures to the Philadelphia Museum. Apparently, this was all true, but then a few months ago he quarrelled with the museum and drew up a new will, leaving the whole thing to me. The lawyer says he might have changed his mind again; he was always changing his mind. But he had a stroke a month ago, and that was it. It was massive, and he died within hours. So the will stands. Isn't it marvellous?''

"Absolutely,'' Rhodine said. Emilia went on explaining. "And it's the pictures that will do the trick. You see, he bought French Impressionist and Post-Impressionist paintings all the time, fifty years ago, and sat on them. He only let a few people see them. You can imagine what they're worth today.''

"And you'll sell them?''

"Yes, one of those huge Sotheby sales. The lawyer was on the phone a few times, but rather vaguely, but finally he flew over on Concorde three days ago and gave me all the details. The Sotheby sale is certain to raise millions, so I can get to work right away. I'm sure the other directors at Aston's will support me, and I don't care what it will cost to buy Cranford out so that I can become chairman like Grandfather.''

"Will he agree to sell? I thought he was so madly keen on publishing.''

Emilia frowned. "Yes, he might be difficult. But surely money will talk. He's that kind of man. Of course it will take a certain time before the sale is through, but I'll be able to raise large sums from the bank in anticipation, so I can do the groundwork now. I'll start discussing things with him immediately, and when he sees how the land lies, it will stop him doing all the terrible things he's said the business needs to become one of the giant publishing houses.''

"What sort of things?''

Emilia had picked up a roll and now tore it apart in anger. "He's had me in to talk of the way he wants to restructure the financial base, and also to look around for other companies in poor state that he can pick up cheaply, taking a few key people from them and sacking our own people who've been with us for years and whom he finds inefficient. Cut back on old stocks and warehousing. Drop some of the new authors and take on more patriotic writers, staunch Conservatives, books on the glories of the Empire, and also books that what he calls "ordinary people" can read the way they used to, nice old stories with clean language and happy endings. We've simply got to stop him. He can do things as chairman without consulting us. If he once gets going, it will be terrible. But there was no way I could see to stop him, no easy way, until I got this news. Now, he'll just have to agree to leave us—sell his stock to me and clear out."

"Have you talked to the other directors yet? Has there been anything in the papers about the will and all that?"

"Not yet. They've kept my name out of it so far because the museum people were threatening a challenge to the will, and the lawyers wanted to see if the museum had some documents or evidence that might stand up in court. But they haven't, so all is in the clear. My lawyer friend says that the museum hasn't got a leg to stand on. He's got a German name, Joseph Hogsheim, and he's a very ardent Protestant; they call it Pennsylvania Dutch. Apart from settling some old scores with the museum, he's very pleased for me to have it because of our anti-IRA book. He hates the Catholics. Besides, he's very romantic about families: long-lost niece inherits fortune from old uncle. My name will be out soon, and there'll be tremendous publicity, he says."

The waitresses were now hovering around them, one with the grilled haddock they had chosen, the other with dishes holding courgettes and salad. Emilia gestured to them to serve, but was too involved with her story to take much notice. Rhodine was less prosaic. "Shouldn't we have a glass of wine?" she said. "Champagne, really. It's so exciting. How can you be so calm about it?"

"I haven't really taken it in yet," Emilia said. "As long as I had to bottle it up I couldn't really believe it; but now . . . you're right. We *must* celebrate."

The wine-waiter was close by, and she called him over. "A half-bottle of champagne," she said to him. Surely that was not too lavish to offend the austere spirit of Grandfather Wren. The waiter, listening to the order, looked down at the haddock. It still wasn't right, but he bowed his head obediently.

Detective Inspector George Green was sitting in a modernish swivel-chair, his feet on a plastic-topped desk, in the depressing room that had been allotted to him in the new Scotland Yard building, which clearly economized on space for mere inspectors. Green was looking after the bomb enquiry for the Anti-Terrorist Branch in the absence of his superintendent, convalescing after an operation. He was, it is true, acting superintendent and expecting promotion. But for the moment he had to take what was offered. As far as possible, he always tried to keep his eyes closed when he sat in this horrible room, with its synthetic light-purple carpet. The famed TV policeman, Dixon of Dock Green, had never had to put up with anyone modernizing the furnishings of his police station. Surely that accounted for the equitable temperament that so delighted his TV audience. In a background of old-fashioned and comfortable squalor, where chipped mugs splashed tea without protest on rickety and scarred tabletops, one had a safe base on which to receive the impact of the horrors flowing in from outside. Here, with imitation elegance imported from the ghastly

21

neon-lit furniture shops of Tottenham Court Road, one was in danger of losing the special authority that flowed from the distinctive aura (a word he might have spat at) of being a hobby. This room was too much like his own kitchen at home.

With eyes closed, then, he was addressing his assistant, intensifying, a bit, his cockney accent in a jokey gesture towards the mellifluous upper-class speech of his new assistant, the recently promoted Detective Sergeant Anthony Piers Tesserel-Brougham. It was really, of course, the *Honourable* Anthony, etc. As the second son of the 11th Viscount Calshott, "the Hon." was there by right, however odd it might look in a fully spelt-out police staff list. Perhaps it had figured with natural ease lower down the educational ladder at Eton and Oxford. Here, it had to be dormant for the space of a few rungs until he had ascended, as surely he would, to the rarefied level of commander or even assistant commissioner, where society and *Private Eye* would make the most of it. Even better if his older brother disappeared at some stage, leaving the title vacant for him. Wasn't British democracy wonderful? The great-grandson of Field Marshal Viscount Calshott, who had saved the army's bacon in his legendary defence of Hadrigar in the Afghan Wars, was free, for a while at least, to walk the streets as simply as Dixon himself: "Good evening, all."

"Do we know anything more about Morgan?" Green was asking. It was now nearly four o'clock. They had been summoned to Aston and Wren's shortly after nine in the morning. Back at New Scotland Yard by eleven, they had launched enquiries in many directions, including a request via the Washington Embassy to the Pentagon to pass on what they knew about the bomb expertise or Mr. Felix Morgan.

"They've confirmed what he said about Vietnam," the sergeant said. "He had a first-class record, with two commendations for bravery in defusing mines under very dangerous conditions. They're going to send us more about his background when they get back to working hours. It was the middle of the night for them, of course."

"Did they say how old he was?"

"Thirty-nine."

"I wonder what he did before he became private dogsbody to Cranford," Green said reflectively. "Quite a job to land."

"Perhaps he went to the Harvard Business School," the sergeant suggested. "They often recruit top-flight business executives from there, and Morgan may just be getting practical business experience this way."

Green opened his eyes and looked at his sergeant quizzically. "Yes, we all know about getting practical experience on the way up, don't we?"

Brougham reddened, but held on firmly. "You didn't want to ask him directly, sir?"

"No, Tony and do drop the 'sir' business, or I won't be able to have a joke with you. I like to ruminate aloud, and 'sir' puts me off. No, I didn't ask him, though I was very curious. There's lots of questions I wanted to ask in that funny old publishing place, but I thought I'd wait to see what surfaced."

Sgt. Brougham was clearly surprised. "You doubt the connection with the IRA? They did tell me about that book, *Evil in the North*. Don't you think that's what started it all off?"

"Oh, I have an open mind about everything," Green said easily. "It makes life more interesting."

"But surely, sir . . . ."

"There's no surely. Anyhow, not until the army lads have matched the bomb with what they pick up in IRA warehouses."

"Commander Winterton seemed so sure it was an IRA design."

"I don't really doubt it," Green said. "It's *got* to be an IRA toy. Buy why shouldn't I ruminate a little? I love ruminating. You'll have to put up with that, won't you?"

"That's no trouble, sir," the sergeant said. "Oh, sorry, sir. I can't get out of it. My last Inspector, in G Division, was a stickler for it. But there's something I did want to ask. It seems obviously an IRA bomb, but there's something bothering you. Is it just a feeling, something you can't define?"

"Yes, Tony, that's about it. It's something Winterton said. Just like the IRA bombs we've had, he said, but worrisome because it was put together just a bit more efficiently. The IRA have obviously got someone down in the workshop who's helping them to make the bombs better, or worse from our point of view. Worrisome, werry worrisome. But that's just one of our troubles, isn't it? We've got to protect his lordship now, haven't we? What have you laid on?"

"I spoke to Morgan about it, and he consulted Lord Cranford. He says he doesn't want any protection. He's quite satisfied with Morgan keeping an eye on things."

Green snorted. "Well that's a lot of cock, and I hope you told him so. If he doesn't want us around, we'll just have to do it without asking. Did you find out what he's doing, where he's going, his wife, and all that?"

"Yes, I got it all out of Morgan. He accepted that it was reasonable. Cranford's going to a reception at the Savoy at six o'clock, given by British Steel. Apparently British Steel have broken a new record."

"For nonproduction, you mean. Okay. Who are you sending there?"

"Constable Fulton, Terry Fulton. Morgan has told him when the car's leaving the UEI building for the Savoy, and he'll follow him."

"And after that? Home to wifey?"

"Home, but not to wifey. Lady Cranford's away in Scotland. She's acting in a play up there. She wanted to fly back when she heard about the bomb, but he told her not to be silly. That's how Morgan put it."

"So all on his own-some tonight, watching the telly?"

The sergeant smiled. "Not quite. He's expecting a visitor for dinner."

"You are smirking. You mean he's expecting a lady?"

"A lady, yes, but Morgan says it's strictly business, so I suppose we have to believe him. At least she won't be some secret IRA agent to murder him in his own bath, like Charlotte Corday."

"Well, that's a relief, if only I knew who Charlotte somebody was. Would you mind very much sticking to the point? Who is this lady visitor?—if you know, that is."

"She's a writer, a historian called Victoria McKenzie. Not an Aston and Wren writer, but very well known. Cranford wants to talk to her about books. She published a big book last year on Kruger."

"There you go again. Who's Kruger? Don't forget I left school at fourteen."

"Sorry, sir. I was no good at history, either, but I did a paper at Oxford on the Boer War. Kruger was a great hero of the Boers; Oom Paul, they called him. Very powerful figure."

"You think she's going to be asked to write a book about Cranford?"

"It did cross my mind."

"Unless, of course, young Mr. Morgan is just fooling us about Miss McKenzie, because he knows that we'll be keeping an eye on comings and goings at the Cranford residence. Where do the Cranfords live, by the way?"

"Chesham Square, when they're in London. Suffolk for the weekends—Pelham Court, near Ashenham.

Pretty big place. I happen to know it because my people live fairly near. My father sometimes went there when it belonged to Lord Tenderden."

"Very nice, very nice. Maybe we'll all get invited there to keep an eye on his lordship. But tonight it's just Chesham Square, I suppose. At least it's better than cruising round the usual IRA safe-houses off the Edgware Road. I wonder if they'll have another go at Cranford. It's best for them sometimes not to have a follow-up when the bomb doesn't go off. Keeps everybody on tenterhooks. Well, I'll leave it all to you." He got out of his chair and stretched himself. "I've got to go to the Home Office about all this. The Assistant Commissioner is coming, too. Quite a little party. I'm sure we'll get a glass of sherry from the Home Secretary or the Permanent Secretary. And I really have nothing to tell them."

"Except your feeling of something unusual . . ."

"Oh, I won't bother them with *that*. That's just my private ruminations, which I utter to whoever is in this revolting room with me. We'll know more tomorrow, I daresay. I'd particularly like to hear more from Washington. Also anything from Suffolk, or anywhere else, especially if it seems to have no relation to the matter in hand. The more you find out from people you run into by accident, the better. The private thoughts of Inspector Green."

"Yes, *sir*," the sergeant said, matching his tone as expected.

At five o'clock exactly, Felix Morgan stepped into a phone booth in the vast lobby of the UEI building, took out some coins, and dialled a number. Far away in Scotland, a woman, standing in a phone booth with her hand protectively over the receiver, waited until it rang a couple of times and then lifted it to her ear. She smiled when she heard the voice.

She was a tall handsome woman, with the air of an Italian beauty, dark-hair, strong features, olive skin. She was wearing a fine black leather coat that was just right for her look of independence, almost disdain.

"All went very well," Morgan said. "Just as expected. Stage two tonight. Stage three in a couple of days. All laid on."

There was a slight pause at the other end, and something uncertain in her voice when she spoke. "So we're there at last, after all these years."

Morgan seemed to want to stick to the practicalities. "The timing is perfect. The people I see have just had a fresh supply. They want me to do a little job for them."

"And the woman tonight, the writer?"

"It's going to be okay," he said. "That was the one loose end: access to the papers, just in case they gave things away. I'll be working on this, and I think it's going to be all right. When are you coming back?"

"What's today? Wednesday, isn't it? Just two more nights. So I'll fly down on Friday morning. I've asked Patrick to come down for the weekend, to rehearse the play scenes." She paused again. "It brings a lot back," she said rather dreamily. "How we got into this, you and I." Her voice had drifted off. "In those days, when we talked, the play was made for us. It seems a bit strange now, acting it out with Patrick. The trouble is, he's so good, so elegant. That Irish elegance is just right. He reminds me so much of Alan Badel. I get absorbed in wondering if we'll do the scenes better than the way they're done in the Shakespeare Company version. I think we will. The setting's better . . . ."

Listening, he felt rather annoyed by the ease in which she floated off to theatre, while counting on him for the cold realities. She was obviously trying to blot out what might happen. "The plan will work," he said, as if stifling his own doubts. "And if not, there's a variant for later that I'm working out. But nothing is going to go wrong."

She was calmer now. "Yes, this is the hard time. But one day . . ."

"Yes, one day." They rang off.

2

VICKIE HAD MADE up her mind to take the flat, with its view across the roofs toward Westminster Abbey, the moment she came through the door, over a year earlier. All the dirt and discomfort of the world were abolished in that view.

It had other good features, including a high ceiling, a large walk-in pantry, and any amount of cupboards. Being high, open, and peaceful, it was a home that encouraged one to take things slowly. She had been working quietly since lunch on a rather absorbing review for the *Spectator,* with everything else blotted out. But now it was six o'clock, and she had to get down to things. She listened to the news on the BBC while she took her bath, but nothing further was being said about the letter-bomb. Feeling pleasantly relaxed, she sat now with a dry martini in her hand, enjoying the sunset light on the Abbey windows, before taking a final decision on the inevitable question: what dress for a tête-à-tête dinner in Chesham Square, with undoubtedly a butler on hand?

It was a question to which she knew, of course, she would find an answer. What name Achilles had assumed when he hid among women, though puzzling, was not beyond conjecture. It was even easier with dresses, since she had only five or six really presentable ones to choose from. She knew that she looked best in a dress that lay low on her shoulders and bosom; both features were so beautifully rounded, Laurence had said. She herself felt feminine and sexy this way. The dark maroon dress would be fine. She was at ease in it.

No real problems there; but what about the book? She had not taken to Cranford at their first meeting. Physically he was very small and, somehow, grubby. Not at all appetising, she had thought. But did that matter for a captain of industry? No one was going to be as tall and impressive as Kruger, that great Old Testament prophet. Very small men often had a radiant dynamism. It might emerge when she knew him better.

She had looked him up in *Who's Who,* and read a page and a half about him in Anthony Sampson's *Anatomy of Britain.* Nothing decisive or unexpected had emerged from the Sampson piece, but there was something in *Who's Who* that drifted through her mind as she looked into the mirror a little later, putting on her makeup. Most of the entry had led nowhere. He was, it seemed, seventy-six, born in Yorkshire with no further details given, "began to work in industry at 14," after which there was an immensely long list of high positions in commerce and industry. But his marriages were surely significant. His first wife—they had had no children—had died in 1973, and six years later he had married, *en secondes noces,* a lady with the divine name of Margaretta Paradiso, of Los Angeles, California. Could that really be somebody's name, Vickie wondered, peering into the mirror. Americans did have funny names, of course; but wasn't this going a bit too far? Morgan had said she was an actress. Perhaps this was just an assumed name that she had taken for the movies and that had then stuck, like Rock Hudson. What would she be like? No hint of her age, of course, in *Who's Who,* but one could guess. He would have been over seventy, so one might safely predict that the beautiful Margaretta would be in her forties or even in her thirties—tall, dark, and Italian—beautifully gowned—splendid in every way.

Vickie felt rather relieved that Lady Cranford was not to be around that night to dinner. The contrast might have been painful. In the old days at Oxford, and later in graduate work and teaching, she had never been in competition, thinking that people probably saw her as a bluestocking, and therefore *hors concours*. Truth to tell, she was not unhappy at how she looked: her little retroussé nose was perhaps even pretty in its way. She seemed to have fine shoulders, according to Laurence, and he had often said that she had an absolutely heartwarming smile. So maybe she was all right. After all, she couldn't hope to look like Sophia Loren. Secretly, she wondered sometimes if she had something of her favourite actress Judi Dench in her looks.

At no point, and to no one, would she have spelt this out. Thoughts just drifted through her mind sometimes, as background to what was really important. And on this occasion, a book might be in the offing. That was important enough in all conscience. She felt a little nervous about it as she got out of the taxi at 6 Chesham Square and rang the bell.

By 9:30, with dinner over, her doubts had vanished. There was certainly a book to be written, and she was the one to write it. The ingredients were all there, she felt it in her bones, and with only one snag: he was alive. If only he were dead, as dead as Kruger, she would let herself go. How was she to deal with it when he was there to watch everything, snapping at her heels like a Yorkshire terrier?

She had said something like this to him, and it was his answer that had won her over.

"Yes, I won't publish it if I don't like it. You'll have the rights, though, in your contract, to publish it when I'm dead if you want to. The main thing is that I want it written so that I can read it while I'm still alive, and by someone really tough like you. I want to see what my life has added up to. *The Times* will give me a long notice, and it wouldn't mean a thing, even if I saw it. Just the public story. Meaningless. I really want to see where the horror fits in."

"Horror? Have you done horrible things?"

"I have. Many horrible things. When I saw what had to be done to get on, I was quite ruthless if I had to be. You may not get on to all the things, and I may not tell you, but you'll find out enough, I'm sure. There were battles and I was going to win them."

He was sipping a brandy, hunched back in his chair. The Yorkshire in his voice had grown rougher. The rich furnishings of the room had ceased to dominate. He was himself at last. This was the real incentive, the real reward: confession. He wanted it spelt out.

"You'll have all my papers," he said, "and I'll put you on to things that you couldn't find in the papers, sharp things, mean things. I don't care how it looks, as long as it doesn't harm anyone except me."

"But you'll keep some things back?"

"And you may find them out."

"I'll have to find my way first."

"That's why you're here. You did it for Kruger, and you were remote enough from him. You're just as remote from *my* world—*more* remote, just because it's a world that looks familiar to you but really isn't until you see the way it operates, or at least the way it was manoeuvred by me. I don't mean that all big businessmen have risen the way I did. Some did, I'm sure. There should be a price to pay. I don't know if I paid it, and I need to know."

Vickie stirred in her chair. "What sort of price? It sounds like *Crime and Punishment*."

He looked at her steadily. It was doubtful if he saw the literary reference, but absorbed it in his own way.

"Yes," he said. "I spent too much time in chapel as a boy not to believe in crime and punishment. It was always the Old Testament for us. Sin was in the air, and the sinner would be punished. You can't imagine how strong this is in me. You were never in chapel, I suppose."

"No, we went to the parish church in our little village in Devon."

"So it was the New Testament. Everything is love. Even love your enemies. Totally impossible. Not just impossible, but sinful to think that there's a way out that way. When a wrong has been done there are consequences, and they will always come through in the end. I believe this for my own life. I sometimes think that I'm in the middle of it right now. Here am I: rich, powerful, title, beautiful wife; but you can't blow evil away. It works its way through."

"Is this the story you want me to tell?"

"In your own way, of course. There are so many ways of telling a story, and I want to see which one you'll choose."

"I never saw myself as the Recording Angel."

"Nor are you. In chapel we expected everything to be written down in heaven. I don't think I'm so flat-footed now. I'm ready to face any way of telling a story. I don't think those idiots at Aston's will ever understand why I'm so absorbed now by books and their possibilities. I don't read a great deal, but every now and then I run into a book that seems to have a very original approach, like that book—I'll say the title in English—'Dangerous Liaisons.' I'm sure you know it."

Vickie was rather startled. "Wonderful book," she said a little lamely. "But—how did it come your way?"

He laughed, enjoying her surprise. "You're as bad as they are. Think all I can read is a balance sheet. Well, I agree it is a bit unusual for me. Actually, my wife,

Margaretta, gave it to me to read. She's an actress, you know, and got the idea of doing some scenes from it at our festival in Suffolk next month. You know about the festival?"

Vickie shook her head. "Oh, it's a great event," he said. "I inherited it when I bought Pelham Court from Lord Tenderden. He'd been running an arts festival there every year in the barn, a great Elizabethan barn, the longest in England. The festival is mostly music, but they've also had lectures and theatrical performances, mostly Shakespeare, with top people performing. She told me about the *Liaison* book and said it could be adapted—scenes from it—for a performance in the barn. Of course it would cost a bit to put on, and that's why she wanted me to read the book, persuade me to put up the cash."

"I think I read about an adaptation recently by the Royal Shakespeare Company," Vickie said.

"Yes, Margaretta was a bit irritated that she's been pipped, but it did confirm her feeling that it was playable. As you know, it's really two main roles. Naturally she wants to do the Marquise, and she has a wonderful Irish actor in mind, she says, for the Viscount. Anyhow, I read parts of the book she showed me. Of course most of it is just boring old-fashioned letters: a lot of rubbish. But the underlying moral is great. These two characters are absolutely evil. They treat human beings with complete cynicism. But it's a highly moral story because in the end they get paid off for their sins. My wife says it's a very elegant book. I can't see that. But I do see how moral it is."

Vickie found herself smiling at the thought of the contrast; the eighteenth-century subtleties of attack and counterattack by the Marquise and the Vicomte, and the majestic takeovers of United Engineering International.

"Am I to write of dangerous liaisons at UEI?" she asked.

"No," he said. "I don't want an imitation of that particular style. But human beings don't change. We have the same motivations, and the same satisfactions. That is constant. You'll tell me things about myself that I didn't know."

"You really are flattering me," Vickie said, "and I love it."

"I think you'll deserve it. In any case, I'm willing to take a chance. There's just one condition that will make it work for me. It's all to be totally secret—I mean the content of the book—until I give the word. You'll have the whole basement here to yourself, where all the papers are stored. I've got a large part of it fitted out as a fine office, locked up with two keys like a safe-deposit. You'll have one key, and my butler, Morrison, will have the other one; the doors open only when they're both used. Nobody else gets in."

Vickie held back from an obvious question. She would have thought that Felix Morgan had access, or at least was involved somehow. She'd had the feeling that he was very close to his employer, and Cranford had spoken of him very warmly when they discussed the bomb scare. But he was to be excluded. A bit odd. But then the whole thing was so odd. Not being commissioned by an industrial chief to write a biography. That was common enough. But this sort of biography—warts and all, with the subject still alive, and with echoes of *Les Liaisons Dangereuses* . . . of course she was going to accept.

"You can talk to all kinds of people," he was saying. "I'll give you their names. People I've worked with, or worked against. Many of them are still around, but some have disappeared. You'll have to track them down. You'll get a few surprises, I dare say. We must talk more fully when you have got into the archives, and you must meet

Margaretta." He took out his diary. "Could you come down for the day in three weeks' time, Saturday, May 17th? I am away at weekends before then."

They went on talking for a while. Before she left, he showed her the basement area, built into the courtyard behind the house, surrounded by a high wall and with the office blocked off by a massive door like, as he had said, a safe-deposit area in a bank. If this had been the world of Choderlos de Laclos there would have been a back door through which the lover escaped from the latest liaison, with the husband rolling up in a chaise at the front door. But this wasn't eighteenth-century France; it was Mrs. Thatcher's England, with business-men called on to enjoy themselves making huge sums of money. Was this how Cranford would appear in her pages? Not very likely. For one thing, it didn't really look as if he had enjoyed himself while he made his pile, despite the bravado he now assumed. Somewhere there was a pretty heavy legacy of guilt, which the book was to expunge. Would she have access to it? Would she be able to express it? A darlint question, as Joxer Daley would have said. A darlint question.

Coming home after an evening like this was when she missed a companion, either Laurence to fall into bed with, or someone to talk to over a final nightcap. Ambrose Usher, either alone or with a group of friends, had always been wonderful in this role, turning the reminiscences of the evening into a stage performance, name-dropping through literature and high society in a rapid flow of benign sophistication. It added to the fun that he was so polished and dapper in the way he dressed, "button-cute" (to borrow S. J. Perelman's phrase) and shoes ashine, a nod to propriety that neatly offset the earthy philosophic views he pretended to link, across seven centuries, with the antischolastic outlook of his

36

Oxford predecessor Duns Scotus. After all, he argued, one breathed the same air, as Gerard Manly Hopkins had said in his loving poem on the old Scot. Oxford—"bell-swarmed, lark-charmed, rock-racked, river-rounded"—loved Ambrose in this vein, and none more than Vickie. How good it would have been, she thought, to have been able to gossip with him after the odd encounter she had had that evening. She had seen a good deal of him when Laurence was in her life, and he always seemed to like her. But he was away, as she had found out when she had phoned his college at a bleak moment after Laurence had gone. The porter had said that he was lecturing in America, and was not due back until early May.

People often said that the "lecturing in America" formula was just a cover for the secret jobs he did in Washington, picking up the trail of earlier years when he had worked on Intelligence at the embassy. Certainly he was in Washington a lot, beyond reach, in any case, to ask him about Cranford, whom he probably knew. He knew everybody.

The bomb story was on page one of *The Times* the next day. Ambrose, staying with Sir Peter Bosworth, one of his oldest pals, who had now returned to the embassy as number two with the rank of minister, saw the paper on the breakfast table as if they were in England. "The time gap plus a new midnight air flight," Carolyn Bosworth explained, noting his surprise.

Carolyn was new, and younger than Peter. Why do I love really English-looking women so much? Ambrose asked himself, reaching out happily from his own Croat background. Born in Uszce, which had given him his Usher name, he was, in fact, totally English in the other authentic way, as the ineradicable alien that the English enjoy putting up with. "There'll always be an England, and I'll always be a foreigner," he would say. "Just a few miles farther south and I would have been an Albanian. Can you imagine it?"

"So just a short visit?" Carolyn was saying. "Too bad. I do so enjoy hearing you and Peter talking about the good old days."

It was their languid quality, Ambrose decided. There wasn't a really languid woman in the whole of Croatia. Not that he was in a position to know, having left Uszce with his parents for London at the age of three. It was the English formula that he knew: languid, and with an air of transparency. When the transparency really worked, as it did with Carolyn, it was like porcelain. And the strange thing was that it often went with a special kind of pure intellect. Look at Dorothy Hodgkin: languid, transparent, and the Nobel Prize for crystallography.

"Of course I have to go back," he said to Carolyn. "After all the excitement, I have to be debriefed over a cup of tea at Richmond Terrace. Ask Peter. They don't ever believe what one tells them in writing. We have to go through the drill in person. Face to face, your true Englishman always shines through."

"You mean like Philby," Carolyn said.

"Exactly. Thousands of reports that he was a phoney, but in person, over a cup of tea at the Terrace, he rang true, as you English put it so felicitously."

Peter looked up from *The Times*. "It's you who are the phoney," he said. "You never tell me half of what you find from your Albanian cousins here. What does King Zog have to say about Enoch Powell? You've probably never even asked."

"You're both impossible," Carolyn said. "Tell me seriously, Ambrose. I don't mean about now but the old times that you and Peter talk about. That murder at the Embassy Guy Fawkes party that they say you solved. Did you go about looking for clues, like Sherlock

Holmes, or is there some sort of process that you count on, and that outsiders like me never hear of?"

"No clues, no magnifying glass, no˙ Dr. Watson," Ambrose declared firmly as he covered his toast lavishly with Oxford marmalade. "I suppose I do know a few people, and they tell me things. They entertain me. I think they want to boast about how much they know now than in the old days. They know I'm easily impressed. I'm gullible."

"Did you say gullible?" Peter asked.

"Well, the stranger is always ready to marvel at new things, even if the natives are blasé."

"What kind of new things?" Carolyn wanted to know. "Can you give an example?"

"Oh yes. Far and away the most startling: the range of what they call the psychofingerprint computer that they've installed at M.I.T. *Time* magazine had an article about it a few months ago. I'm working on computer studies up there myself on philosophy and language, but they let me feed in some straight informational questions to see how connections could be broadened. One day we'll be able to track down everybody, everywhere, if other countries are able to computerize their records to U.S. standards. Of course, things can take a little time to work through. After all, they deal with multitemporal as well as multilingual factors. But they did come through with many of the links I was looking for. Fabulous."

Peter was listening with what might have been amusement, but maybe it was all old-hat to him. "I don't think software is what counts with you," he said. "You're good at asking questions, to loosen things up. Yes, you're quite good."

"Is that it, Ambrose?" Carolyn asked. "Lots and lots of questions?"

Ambrose, mouth full of toast, mumbled a kind of denial. "Not *lots* of questions: a few unexpected ones, maybe. The police take care of the ordinary questions. I suppose I enjoy looking for something else." He broke off suddenly to issue a mock protest. "What is all this third degree? Can't a man keep his secrets? I rest my case. Let me just look at *The Times* to see who's died, before I go off to see my Mafia pals. The Albanian Mafia, of course."

The obit page occupied him only for a second. "What's the matter with everybody in England? No one dead. I think they're still sitting in the same armchair at the Athenaeum and no one has noticed." His eye was now on page one, where he saw the Aston and Wren bomb story under the heading: IRA THREAT TO LORD CRANFORD? The IRA had not yet claimed the bomb, *The Times* said, hence the question mark. But everybody assumed it.

"What a nice little episode," Ambrose said, scanning the story quickly. "No explosion, no one killed, heroic bomb expert wins everyone's admiration, and I see he's American, which is good for Anglo-American relations. Every prospect pleases, except one."

"What's that?" Carolyn asked.

"Why, we still have Lord Cranford among us. It's like a new Glinka opera: *A Life for the Multi-Nationals! Long Live United Engineering!*"

"What have you got against Cranford?" Peter asked. "I thought he was a model citizen: self-made, vast employer, and now a publisher, according to the story."

"That's the part I don't like," Ambrose said. "I've never met him, and he's probably kind to his children and grandchildren, but books! Don't we need someone who *reads* books?"

"How do you know he doesn't?" Peter asked.

"Touché, touché. I don't. He's probably going through Proust for the third time."

"What a snob you are," Carolyn said. "He may be a

marvellous man. This American who defused the bomb seems to have thought it worthwhile saving him."

"I withdraw. What more can I say? I'll make it my business to look into it as soon as I get back, and you shall have a report pronto."

"How would you tackle it if you were given the case?" Carolyn asked. "I mean tracking down the villain. Not lots of questions, you say. Just a key question. What would it be? The IRA is too obvious, so you must find some other angle. What do you think? A business rival? A jealous husband who knows how to make bombs?"

"No," Ambrose said. "All also too obvious. It's the American we have to think of. What did it say his name was? Ah yes: Felix Morgan. All right. Why is he assistant to Lord Cranford? Where does he come from? Does he play chess? Is he attractive to women—or men? Now these are real questions. Shall I take the case?"

"I'm very disappointed in you," Carolyn said, getting up to put the breakfast dishes on a tray. "You're reducing everything to practical questions. I thought you would approach things more deeply. After all, you teach philosophy at Oxford. Isn't there some deep philosophical principle that you can apply to murder, or attempted murder? Not an obvious one, because you hate the obvious, but something no one thinks of as a prime motivation?"

Ambrose, listening to her, was putting on a look of sheer adoration. "But of course," he said. "All the obvious motivations are inadequate. Like cupidity, or jealousy, or chronic irritability, where the wife takes up the kitchen breadknife for the deed because she can no longer stand the sight of her husband picking his teeth with a fork. These obvious ways do catch murderers, I agree. But the one big motive doesn't really surface enough. Revenge: that's the one I like. We should get back to the Middle Ages. The unforgiveable insult. The sword is drawn. The villain falls. So neat and tidy."

"How serious are you?" Carolyn asked. "Why have you suddenly picked on revenge?"

"Out of the air," Ambrose said. "Just feel in my bones that the next case is going to be on revenge."

"All right, I give in," Carolyn said. "You are impossible. There's nothing I can do with you. But don't go home yet. Stay on for a week or two. I like breakfast this way."

But breakfast was over. Ambrose went off, no one knew where, and three days later he was back at his college in Oxford.

3

WARREN FAVERSHAM HAD rung Sekelis in Suffolk after getting back to the office from lunch with Corby. Sekelis, as it happened, was coming to town two days later. They met, as it were, by chance among the tourists wandering round the endless shopping stalls in the new Covent Garden market, and sat down for a drink at a safe distance from the throng.

"I had a word this morning with Pierre," Sekelis said. "They were alerted separately. In fact they thought that the man asking those questions in the pub was being obvious deliberately, to see if it might trigger off a few messages that they could latch on to. Of course I didn't phone you from home: no point in making it too easy. Have you anything else that fits in, especially about Lord Cranford? They still feel sure that something will turn up there among the papers he got from Lord Tenderden."

George Sekelis was a former Bulgarian who now kept an antiques shop in the pretty Suffolk town of Ashenham. He did very well there, especially with tourists on a day's outing to Lyddiham Abbey, dominating Ashenham, and very popular for its turrets and gargoyles. George had slipped into England, with some others of the same Russian allegiance, during the inflow of Hungarian refugees in 1956. He was of medium height, rather dark, with twinkling eyes and the most charming of foreign accents, immensely popular with the locals for his jokey, ever-smiling ways. Though he didn't actually play cricket for the local team, he was an ardent patron, accompanying them always when they were engaged in needle matches with neighbouring villages like Lazenby or Little Gernham, and regularly dropping in, and standing his rounds, at the Pelham Arms. He had been in touch with Faversham soon after his arrival in England, and was the link for messages when needed.

"I've seen nothing in Cranford," Faversham said. "He seem to be throwing himself into publishing purely as a business, or rather as a hobby. He did ask me for an author for a book he wants written, but my impression was that it would be a ghosted book about his business. He talked about having masses of papers that had to be sorted out."

"I suppose he keeps them in London," Sekelis said. "It's the ones at Pelham Court that we're interested in. It's quite certain that Lord Tenderden had got hold of some stuff through Gerald Masterson. The question is: did Tenderden pass it on to MI5 or hold it for his own use? It seemed best at the time to get Masterson out of the way. We didn't know then that he'd put things on paper and given it to Tenderden."

"You've been lucky so far," Faversham said. "Tenderden being so old; I think he was ninety-two when he died. I know he'd always had a great feud in the House of Lords with the Lord Chancellor about his own estate, or his title, or something. Probably wanted to hit the government with a denunciation on not uncovering 'all those spies.' " Faversham was smiling, but not very happily. "And then he died—of moral indignation, no doubt. The Masterson papers may still be there. I expect he had masses of archives. Couldn't we get access?" This time he smiled more broadly. "Why don't you get in yourself? You might be able to pick up a few portable antiques at the same time, say a brooch or two, or some delectable snuffboxes."

"I'm glad you can laugh about it," Sekelis said. "You

seem to forget that your own name is likely to turn up. Michael Pratt got pretty close to you in his last diatribe about Roger Hollis as a secret agent."

"I haven't forgotten," Faversham said sombrely. "Well, not quite. The truth is that I do forget for stretches of time. It's such a long time ago. And then something blows up and brings it all back."

"Well, if you're prepared to sit back and ride the storm, Pierre isn't. And he assumes you'll want to help to cover things up if you can. I don't think the headlines would do you any good. Pierre thinks we must move quickly, just in case the papers at Pelham Court start opening up. Suppose Cranford has caught sight of them. After all, he's a publisher, isn't he? He might want to have another book done, not on his business but on these—what do they call them—'revelations?' You say you haven't seen any sign of it?"

"None at all. I don't think he's really motivated about books. After all, he's lived in another world. I expect one book's the same as another for him, as long as it's profitable. But yes: there is one thing. He's very conservative and patriotic. Revelations might appeal to him and would also be profitable. Yes, I'm sure you're right. You've got to get your hands on the Masterson papers before they're rumbled. I suppose during the week, while Cranford's in London. Are you thinking of having a go?"

Sekelis sipped his beer reflectively. "We've had a go already," he said.

Faversham sat up sharply. "Then what are we talking about?"

"I sent a man in last week. Pretty skillful. No problem in getting into the house—just the butler and his wife looking after things. But the section of the house, a big office, where he must keep the papers, I suppose archives too, is a fortress. Strong doors, big locks: like a safe-deposit in a bank. I've decided that the only way to get into this part of the house is when he's around himself. Take him by surprise when the whole area might be opened up for his own access. And I've thought of a good time to try—during the festival.''

"What festival is that?''

"Lord Tenderden used to have an annual arts festival in the Long Barn—huge Elizabethan barn—in late May, and Cranford's keeping it going this year. Mostly music and lectures, sometimes plays—short ones—some art exhibits, a bit of folk dancing, fireworks, and all that sort of thing. The locals go from the whole area, our cricket team puts on a friendly match, lots of visitors everywhere. I imagine that security will be strong on the barn, especially after that IRA bomb, but that might leave the house itself less well guarded, so that we might be able to get into the safe-deposit area, especially at one point in the evening . . .''

Faversham broke in. "I'll guess. You mean during the fireworks? You could let off a nice bang during the fireworks. No one would notice . . .''

"Yes," Sekelis agreed. "That was one idea. But it might work in a less planned way. I could send someone in to look round at different times in the day. We might just be lucky.''

Faversham looked a little uneasy. "You're not thinking of a little persuasion? I won't say violence? You mean just look for an open door.''

Sekelis was beginning to get a little impatient. "There's no need to spell things out. No one's going to ask *you* to do anything. We just want to get hold of anything that might lead to trouble. As for persuasion— who can tell? One hopes for the best, but things develop by themselves. Where you can help us is on the book side. If he drops any hints that he might already have had a look at this stuff and is just sitting on it for the moment, it would be good to know. Pierre would like to know. You'll ring me if you hear anything.''

He got up ready to leave and looked around before going off. "I'll leave you here. Good place to meet," he said rather jovially, back to the image of the twinkling Sekelis so popular with his cricket-mates at the pub. "Very convenient spot this is: Bow Street Police Station on the left, Opera House on the right.''

"Which are you expecting to visit tonight?" Faversham asked.

"Oh, the opera, of course. The new production of *The Marriage of Figaro*. Why else do you think I came to London today?''

Faversham sat on as Sekelis sauntered off, stopping here and there as a happy tourist, and radiating goodwill in all directions

Emilia had been badgering Felix Morgan for several days to get an appointment with Lord Cranford. She was told that he was in Germany on business, but now he was in the building, at the unearthly hour of 9:15, and she was on her way in to the legendary office on the first floor: Grandfather's office, and surely one that a Wren would occupy again when everything had been arranged.

The Philadelphia lawyer had been on the phone to her several times, asking if she wouldn't come out quickly to see everything on the spot. The trustees would pay for the trip on Concorde, and when she said that she'd like to bring a friend with her—Rhodine, of course—they instantly agreed. They were immensely keen to secure an early date for the Sotheby auction. It was public knowledge that the museum had lost the pictures, though the actual inheritor had not yet been named. Everyone was sure that the news would break soon, with enormous publicity following.

Keen as she was herself to get the arrangements moving, there were things to be done at the English end that had to come first. For one thing, Rhodine wasn't free to go for a few days, having to work through the reports she had made on her trip to the Far East. Emilia was determined to take her along. The excitement would be doubled, trebled, with Rhodine there to share it; and there was something else that made Rhodine's presence absolutely essential. One job that lay ahead was taking decisions on which of the pictures would be held out of the sale. Her first idea, which she still held, was that the museum should be offered a choice of four or five to atone, at least in part, for the loss of the whole collection. Emilia knew nothing about painting, whereas Rhodine was immensely knowledgeable. Her path into advertising had been a kind of sequence to three years at the up-in-front art school, St. Martin's, under the tutorship of the rumbustious Joe Tilson. Her own raffish style of painting was very St. Martin's, but she was knowledgeable about painting in broader terms, ideal to be at Emilia's side in all the discussions. Privately, Emilia had already decided that she was going to invite Rhodine to pick one painting—any one she liked—for herself, the kind of present—perhaps a Renoir or Matisse—that no one could ever give normally. Before the museum got in, she would ask Rhodine which was her favourite of the whole collection, and then say: "It's yours." She hoped it would turn out to be the most valuable painting of all; that would be marvellous. But in a way it would be equally wonderful if Rhodine picked a work by someone little known. It would make the gift really personal between them.

Coming down from her pokey little office on the second floor to see Cranford, she rehearsed things slightly. She wouldn't be telling him about the inheritance, so it was too early yet to hint at the ultimate move. She would have to wait on that until she had the full support of her

48

fellow directors, and that could only be after her return from the Concorde trip, when the news would have come out. What she would get from seeing Cranford now was a guide to how he was going to react when she put her cards on the table. In principle she was sure he could be manoeuvred into resigning. After all, he had no background in books, and if he liked the connection, they might engineer a dignified nonexecutive title like "president," leaving the actual work—and Grandfather's office—to her as chairman.

The excuse she had given Morgan had been that she wanted to start a wholly new series of books that she would tell Lord Cranford about when she had her talk with him. The idea was genuine enough and had come to her when she had been going through some of the backlist surviving from Grandfather's day. It had suddenly struck her that a great many of these once-best-selling authors were women who had now been virtually forgotten. Feminist publishers were already doing very well, but Aston and Wren's backlist in this field was infinitely richer. She herself would choose and edit. Surely this would win him over a bit, on the road to seeing her as managing director if and when he was willing to be bought out.

She had her usual pang as she went in, seeing the familiar Covent Garden church tower through the window. It was on the tip of her tongue to say something, but she held herself back very firmly. She had to play this one very carefully. Did he in fact know of her connection with this room? He must certainly have been told that she was the last surviving Wren descendant when he had come into the business, but he had never referred to it since and had probably forgotten it. Just like him, she thought bitterly, but then shook herself. It would be wrong to let her feelings run away with her.

"Ah, Miss Marritt. Emilia, isn't it? I'm sorry I

couldn't see you earlier. Felix Morgan told me you'd been rather keen to launch a new idea, but he didn't tell me what it was. I take it it's something that hasn't come up yet at one of the directors' meetings."

He was polite enough but rather brusque, as if he was already thinking it a waste of time to expect new ideas to emerge from this rather old-fashioned director, and a woman at that. "Oh, it's not all that urgent," she found herself saying rather defensively. At the same time she suddenly remembered the bomb. "Was it a shock—the bomb, I mean?" she added lamely.

What a strange effect this man had on one. He was waving his hand dismissively in response to her question. He indicated the chair. She decided to go ahead as calmly as she could. It was surely just his business style, where he dealt with projects costing millions of pounds, so unlike the world of publishing, which, it was always said, was a profession for gentlemen.

"It's a new series I've been working out," she said. "I think it could be a great success, especially for us, because we have the material to hand in abundance, and it's been lying dormant, unused, for years."

He was listening intently enough, grey eyes fastened on her. "What kind of material are you thinking of?" he asked.

"It's Victorian and Edwardian," she said. "Very exciting novels, or at least exciting at the time . . ."

"And we should start reviving them," he said, with a distinct touch of sarcasm coming into his voice. "You think that they belong to today."

"They would be a revelation," she said. "People today are waiting for this, especially women . . ."

She had fallen at the first hurdle. She guessed that anything feminist would be anathema to him, and had meant to give this a miss. But now she was down.

"So we have to live on the past," he was saying, with

an open sharpness becoming stronger. "You mean the kind of thing your grandfather used to publish."

So he did know, and resented it. She kept calm, becoming even a little aggressive herself: "Not because they're old, but because there's a new understanding of the woman's world. It's been buried; time to open it up. It's like a new side of literature. People who know about books . . ."

His eyes had narrowed. "Not me, of course," he said. "I'm just an outsider. I can't possibly know . . ."

"Oh, I didn't mean . . ."

"No, of course not." Sarcasm was now in full flow. "I should just let you all go ahead, keep out of your way, shouldn't I? Do you know, I'm very glad you put up this idea. I've sensed the hostility, and it's good to get it brought out." He leaned forward, tapping the tabletop with a finger to add a special kind of toughness to what he had to say. "I expect you're speaking for the others, too. Warren Faversham's been looking down his nose. I can give you a message to pass on. It's just not going to happen . . ."

Emilia sat speechless. She had just wanted to test things without upheaval, and she was getting the answer clearly enough.

"I'm not an idiot," Cranford was saying. "I haven't come into publishing as a hobby, or as a joke. I happen to be very serious about books. I'm not here to coast along. I have some very special projects of my own to push forward, things that mean a lot to me personally. . . ."

Emilia remembered a rumour in the office that he was commissioning a history of his company. Warren Faversham seemed to think so. Was that what he meant? It sounded ominous now, with his temper rising.

"We'll talk about it some other time," he said, rising

to his feet. "I'm calling a meeting for a week from Friday, May 9th." She rose too, and stood facing him.

"Surely nothing in my proposal would go against any of your own projects," she said. "We all want the books we do to mean something personally."

"But you're all so conservative, so old-fashioned," he said testily. "I want to wake you all up, to startle you. I'll give you one example of what I mean. A mass of new material has come my way on how the upper classes in this country gave active support to Russian communism. I call that treachery. We've seen some of it exposed, but there's much more to be told, and I'm going to do it. None of your women's stuff. I want anger in my books. The blood's got to flow. And if you feel that all this doesn't belong in this room"—he waved his arm around with a clear reference to Grandfather Wren—"well, that will be just too bad." He stopped for a moment, feeling, perhaps, that he had been too rude. "Think about it," he said, as if withdrawing the dagger slightly. "You know, I like running this company. I'm going to enjoy bringing it to life again."

Emilia got out of the room almost without saying goodbye. He had thrown her out, in effect. Certainly thrown out her plans. This was not a man who was going to step aside. His contempt for her—and for Grandfather! He was ruthless, evil. This was how he'd built up his fortune, and Aston's was now to become part of it. She felt a surge of hate inside her, something she had never known before. "I could have killed him," she told Rhodine that night. "The measly little horror! If I'd had a gun . . ."

She had sobered down by this time and could talk of it without trembling all over. Rhodine had calmed her, as she always did. It was late now, with a happy evening behind them. The marvel of Rhodine was that she went along with anything one felt, accepting it all, and with laughter part of the soothing process.

"You *should* kill him," she said to Emilia. "Or anyhow, get him killed. We just have to organise it. You'll obviously never get him to agree to step down, however much cash you produce. So we have to find a more direct method to get him out of the way. I'm going to have a little more brandy. Come on, have a little, too. We've got to plan things."

Emilia took some brandy. It felt good. Everything about Rhodine felt good. "All right," she said. "How do we organise it? Let's enjoy the thought anyhow, even if it's impossible."

"Why is it impossible?" Rhodine wanted to know. "It's perfectly possible. It's happening all the time. Don't you read the papers?"

"Of course I do. But all we hear about is when someone has a go and is caught. I've no wish to get caught."

"You're missing the point," Rhodine said. "We read about the failures in the papers, but that just shows how widespread it all is now. A few get caught and we read about them, but lots get through. I'm not talking about brute murder, crimes of passion, and all that. They just give themselves away. I mean those that are planned in a really businesslike way, on a contract. You want someone out of the way: you get an expert to do it, if you have enough cash. Everyone's happy except the poor bloke what's hit on the head, but he probably deserved it."

Emilia had cheered up. The brandy, maybe, or Rhodine's happy acceptance of everything. "And you think you can organise it?" she said to her.

"I haven't the faintest idea how to," Rhodine said. "But I know there are experts in the business. Always go to an expert. It's the amateurs who make a mess of things. Of course, some pros do too—that's how we know it all goes on. Like that case in the papers last week of a woman who'd hired a man—not her lover, but a pro—to get rid of her husband. I forget how they were caught. Something stupid they forgot. But I bet there are people who do these things quite calmly for the cash, plus a certain thrill, I daresay, of doing the job well, like winning the Twenty-Four-Hour Le Mans."

"And where do you find these expert motorists?" Emilia wanted to know.

"You ask around," Rhodine said, calmly enough. "Of course you won't find them among your nice timid publishers, or downstairs here in Kensington. But they're two a penny in Chelsea, or better still in Fulham. Hey! I've just realised how I can find you an operator. Roop. He would know."

"Who's Roop?"

"Haven't I told you about Roop? He's delicious, and he's a very good painter."

"Oh, you mean Rupert Mandeville. He works in your office."

"Roop is fabulous," Rhodine said, helping herself to a little more brandy. "He was at Eton, you know, before I met him at St. Martin's. He just puts on the cockney accent, but it's really his lifestyle that gets him everywhere. He'll know just where to go for murder English style."

"You mean the drug world?"

"Oh, a little more interesting than that, where our true English mafia, say the Hackney lot, meets the Sloane Rangers. It's an open world if you know where to go, as Roop does: all the crooks and the sharp boys, where everything has a price. It's so funny because at the office he works quite hard for a few hours—wonderful work—and then he's off. He's taken me with him sometimes, but of course he has other tastes. Still, he likes me. In fact he's often dolled me up when he's taken me along because I'm so pretty-pretty."

"And he'll find us our man?"

"Absolutely," Rhodine cried. "In his world, someone like Roop comes your way, asks a few questions, and the job gets done. The money has to be manoeuvred, of course, but you'll have plenty of money now, more than you need. Shall I have a word with him? I won't mention any names, of course, I can be the link for the cash—just me and Roop, no connection with you. We'll just have a contract set up, like in the movies. . . ."

She broke off in delight at an idea that had just struck her. "Of course! We could get an American to do it. We'll bring him back when we go on our trip. Roop will give us the right introductions. They all know each other."

Emilia was trying to keep up. "You mean Andy Warhol—those people—"

Rhodine laughed. "Oh, much further out, I'm sure. He's bound to know Warhol, but he's too respectable for what you need. Something very anonymous, and very cool. A baby-faced monster. Roop will get it organised, and pretty soon you'll be back in your grandfather's office, all yours this time."

Emilia sighed. "You are wonderful," she said to Rhodine, taking her hand. "What would I do without you?"

Vickie looked at Ambrose across the luncheon table with great content. He had rung her after his return from Washington, finding the message she had left for him with the college porter. He had no idea when he called that she was involved peripherally with the bomb story he had read about over breakfast with the Bosworths. He had just assumed that she wanted to get a little comfort from him over Laurence's departure to his new post at Brisbane University.

55

"I can guess how you feel," he had said. "A bit ruffled, I expect. Well, Ambrose is around again. All will be well. I'll be in London on Monday. Are you free for lunch?"

"Just what I'd hoped for," she said happily. "As a matter of fact, I had something very practical in mind when I rang. I'd been offered a lectureship at Bristol and wanted your advice. But that has all flown out of the window since then."

"A better offer? Writing another book?"

"Well, yes, like in *The Godfather*. An offer I can't refuse."

"With a bit more danger than in Bristol?"

"Ambrose, you always hit it. Danger is right there. A bomb has been thrown . . ."

"Not the bomb that I read about in *The Times* last week, aimed at Lord Cranford? Wait a minute. Let me work it out. Lord Cranford. Publishing. You're going to do a book for Aston and Wren."

"Warmer and warmer. I'll keep it to tell you when we have lunch. Where will you take me? Somewhere from one of your spy stories, very mysterious?"

"Oh, no. You wouldn't like that. The spies themselves are all members of the Athenaeum, like Sir Anthony Blunt, or hiding out in some obscure pub in Holloway, like where they have those horrible lunchtime plays. Is there one on now that you want to see? No, we have to talk. L'Escargot will be right. It's corny enough by now. Shades of Burgess and Maclean still hang in the air."

She hadn't been there for some time, and was relieved to see that the ceiling lights were still festooned with those absurd tassels. She had begun to tell the story while they sipped an introductory glass of Chambery. Without prearrangement, they had kept off the subject of Laurence. Cranford and his book were far more engrossing. The idea of a safe-deposit style or archive store to herself in a Chesham Square courtyard intrigued him immensely, but he was also very taken with what she told him about this mysterious American, Felix Morgan, who was right at the heart of things with Cranford yet not part of the safe-deposit sanctum. "Tell me more about him," he said.

"I had lunch with him yesterday," she said. "I'd only met him briefly before that, when Cranford had asked me to call at Aston's to discuss the book. He's very engaging; grows on one very nicely. He's tall and fair— American but in the English style, nice and relaxed. He still plays down defusing the letter-bomb. Says it was quite easy after Vietnam."

"How did he happen to go to work for Cranford?"

"I asked him that myself. He says it was through being introduced in America by an American businessman. Cranford had told this man that he was looking for someone with an American business background but who wouldn't be too aggressively American; would fit in easily with English business but never be seduced by the idea of being totally British. Cranford wanted someone to protect him from the rear, so to speak. Morgan had been trained at the University of Chicago Business School, and was working for a big Italian firm in Chicago. I mean Italian-American, of course. The head of the firm had become a good friend of Cranford, and recommended Morgan to him to work as a kind of troubleshooter, not so much in the publishing firm, which is very minor in business terms, but in big deals, mergers and the like. I'm expecting him to be very useful to me when I start working on my book."

"He'll collaborate with you?"

"Well, oddly not," Vickie said slowly. "I was a bit surprised, in fact, at Cranford keeping him out of the talk I had with him; but I realised that the book was very personal to him. He could trust me with his secrets, the way people will trust a psychiatrist, but he didn't want someone involved who was dealing with his real business affairs."

"Do you mean he particularly excluded Morgan . . ."

"Not just Morgan—everybody. He made it a condition that I wasn't to talk about anything from the private papers, which of course I accept. I think that Morgan himself was a bit offended at this."

"Did he bring it up when you had lunch?"

"Well, he said at one point that he wanted to help, and I could turn to him for background, especially on the Chicago side, where Cranford's pal has the lovely name of Frederico Masolino."

"Sounds like a member of the Mafia."

"Yes, that's what *I* thought. But he also wanted to talk about the earlier period in Cranford's life before he became huge and multinational. I said that Cranford didn't seem to want this, and he turned it into a kind of joke, implying that young people like him and me could be in touch easily in ways that older people like Cranford wouldn't understand."

"Was this some sort of come-on?" Ambrose asked. "Did you feel attracted?" It was an oblique way of bringing up the whole Laurence business without mentioning it. It was because of Laurence that they were having lunch. He was a ghost of the feast. She had to expunge him; they both knew it, and it would happen not through words of comfort or argument but by coming to life in a new way. Cranford's book project was already working this change. Ambrose could feel it. Morgan might be another living element. It would be interesting to see if she herself recognised this. She was smiling a little at his question. Her smile was very engaging, Ambrose thought. It really transformed her.

"I think he'd be rather a handful," she said. "One feels there's an awful lot behind him that one wouldn't get hold of easily. But I don't know. Does one always have to know everything about a person to enjoy them? Take you. You're a real man of mystery. Everybody says so. But you're very nice to be with. Morgan's the same.''

"Oh, I resent that," Ambrose protested. "I like to think I'm unique."

"And so you are," Vickie said, stretching out a hand across the table to rest on his. "How could you think otherwise?"

It was good, she felt. Laurence was vanishing into thin air. What a bastard he'd been. Life was going on happily without him, as if a tapestry of pleasure was being woven. The dinner with Cranford had been an unexpected delight. Morgan at lunch was intriguing in a different way, opening up a personal friendship in a way one discovers a new novelist—not necessarily a world-shaker but someone with a fresh mind. She would see more of him. He had suggested it, and she was ready. As for Ambrose, seeing him now without Laurence in the background was intensely pleasant; the perfect confidant one wanted to be close to.

"Did Morgan tell you if the police had found out anything more about the bomb—who sent it and all that?" he was asking. "They might confide in him, as he's such an expert."

"The police got a message, but not from the IRA," Vickie said. "They have some sort of code for dealing with the IRA. This message was from a new organization which called itself PRA, People's Revolutionary Army. More Marxist, they think. They'll soon be finding out more from their agents. Morgan said the police know far more than they tell the public. He said that they would know much more by the time of the festival. He would tell me what he heard."

"What festival is that?"

She laughed. "Aren't you performing at it? It's a very

Oxbridge affair in Suffolk. I would have thought they might have roped you in for a lecture, but obviously not. It's at Pelham Court, where Lord Cranford lives. It used to belong to old Lord Tenderden, who died last year. There's a vast Elizabethan barn where Tenderden used to stage an annual arts festival, recitals, lectures, and all that. Cranford's continuing it this year, largely to please his wife, who's an actress. They always put on some play: scenes from Shakespeare, or something like that. This year they're doing an adaptation of *Les Liaisons Dangereuses*. She's performing, of course, with a small cast. I'm invited up there and of course I'll go. It's at the end of May. Why don't you come up?"

"Pelham Court. Yes," Ambrose said. "I remember now. Our music Fellow told me that the Guarneri Quartette are going there to play some chamber music. But it's rather a long way to go to hear a little late Beethoven."

"Oh, do come," Vickie said, suddenly keen to drop the banter and have him around for help. "Do come, Ambrose. I need you a little, you know. I won't be a pest, but I'd like you to be there. Will you come?"

"On second thoughts," Ambrose said, "it's never too far to go to hear late Beethoven. I'll get them to play Opus 135: *Muss es sein? To Be or Not to Be*. It will solve all our problems, won't it?"

"Oh, darling Ambrose." She suddenly felt very warm toward him. "I knew you'd help me, and you have. I have a feeling that things will come up that I'll want to ask you about. I'll have got into the book by then, or at least into the background reading. It will be like having a tutorial, but where can I get a tutor like you?"

"Where, indeed?" Ambrose grunted contentedly, as they got ready to leave.

At home she picked up Roseveare's massive book, *The Treasury*, which she'd just got out of the London Library. She'd taken it out to see if it helped her to understand the government's attitude in not promoting industrial expansion before the war. She'd thought it might have come up in talking to Ambrose; not that he was an expert, but somehow one felt more likely to understand anything—even treasury policy—after talking to him. Darling Ambrose, she thought, as she settled down with Roseveare.

Visits to Scotland Yard from FBI men were frequent enough; the Yard still had its own cachet for them. This one still sounded as if he might be rather special, if only because his name was going to be hard to get round one's tongue: Ignazs Szybalnunczki—number two, it seemed, in the huge section devoted to business fraud. Sergeant Brougham was bringing him in at 11:30. Inspector Green had already been partially briefed and was looking forward to a meeting which had surfaced purely by accident.

Szybalnunczki's name had come up while Sergeant Brougham had been looking round for information from U.S. sources about the knowledgeable bomb-man Felix Morgan. One followed up everything and everybody when one worked on anti-terrorism. Morgan had acted brilliantly, certainly avoided a big bang at Aston and Wren's, and perhaps saved Lord Cranford's life. The Pentagon had readily confirmed that he had been a bomb specialist in Vietnam, with high honours for bravery. Asked if they would expand on this, they had volunteered, from their normal followup records, that he had gone to the University of Chicago with his veterans's grant and graduated with distinction. From there, the army record grew fainter; but the business school noted that he'd got a good appointment immediately with the Illinois Traction Company. The followup there had taken him to Mercantile Universal of Ohio, from where he had moved to United Engineering International of England, as special assistant to Lord Cranford at a high salary. The personnel chief at Mercantile thought that the salary at UEI was less significant than the broadening of experience in moving to London, with its rapidly expanding importance in the financial world through the EEC. He'd got the job because the head of Mercantile, Frederic Masolino, who thought highly of Morgan, had wanted to do Cranford a good turn, and it had taken this form. There'd been talk at the time of a big merger, with UEI moving into a takeover position.

All this was routine and had become freely available in a few days of enquiry through the agent whom Scotland Yard kept regularly in Washington. None of this had any obvious reference to antiterrorism until a slight but faintly possible link to bombs surfaced through a scandal that had just erupted around Frederic Masolino, the man who had introduced Morgan to Cranford. The highly respectable Frederic—or Frederico—had been called before a grand jury in Ohio looking into Mafia incursions into big business. The Scotland Yard agent in Washington had passed this on apropos Morgan, together with a practical suggestion that might ease further enquiries. The FBI man watching the case before the grand jury, a highly placed officer called Ignazs Szybalnunczki, was on his way to London that very week and would gladly drop in at Scotland Yard to see Detective Inspector Green. Things could sometimes be said in person to colleagues about the top people in big business that one couldn't put down on paper. Detective Sergeant Brougham had made the arrangements through a well-briefed man at the U.S. Embassy in London. Green was looking forward to the meeting, especially after he'd learnt from Brougham that the pronunciation of the name offered no real difficulty. The surname was eased into

Zebansky in conversation. Better still, he was known universally as Zeb. No problems.

Why were Americans so big and fat? Zeb, fair and huge, practically filled the little office when Brougham brought him in. Luckily, the hideous modern chair he fell into was the typical tubular monstrosity that now pervaded all branches of the Civil Service but was able, at least, to take heavy weights entrusted to it. Zeb exuded affability on a grand scale as his great palm enfolded Green's hand.

"Well. New offices," he said with a rather twinkling look around the crowded room with its purple carpet. "I visited the old building a couple of years ago. Quite different, isn't it? I expect you miss the old atmosphere: Sherlock Holmes period and all that."

They chatted on this for a moment, becoming George and Zeb instantly, before turning to the subject on hand. "I don't think I can help you," Zeb said. "All I really know is about balance-sheets: not a thing about bombs."

"But the Mafia," Green said. "We always prick up our ears. Have to. Is this Masolino man really linked to it, and could that spill over to other contracts?"

"You mean to Lord Cranford and UEI?" Zeb asked rather teasingly. "We mustn't infect you, must we?"

"You know how it is, Zeb," Green said. "We just follow things up, the way you do, without expecting anything to come out in the immediate case. Why is the Ohio Grand Jury into this? Is it a corruption story which might have overflowed here?"

"No, it's a very different approach," Zeb said. "We've begun to take the Mafia backing in regular business for granted now. They've been laundering everything, diversifying, buying in on a huge scale; but every now and then some hyperactive district attorney decides he'll pursue the story, mainly for his own political reasons, so we get launched into grand juries and Senate committee hearings. Sometimes the businessman falls by the wayside, but usually they know how to take care of themselves."

"Even when we hear of all kind of dirt coming out, plus Mafia bumping-offs?"

"We don't care for the bumping-offs, especially when it's an act of persuasion and not just revenge. We don't like that. But most of the bloodletting is within the family, so to speak. A lively D.A. goes after it if he can, but it doesn't usually affect the conduct of business, which is *my* interest. However, if some link does come through I'll let you know, of course."

"Could I raise something?" Sergeant Brougham asked. "In all this diversifying, does the leadership stay Italian, or do they mix it up? I mean this Frederic Masolino is presumably Italian, but he was very fond of Morgan, you say, and did a great favour to him by introducing him to Lord Cranford. But to our ear, Morgan sounds Welsh. Is there a Welsh Mafia to do each other favours, which might spill over into bloodshed now and then?"

Zeb laughed. "We're not quite as ethnic as all that," he said. "But it's true. There are all kinds of mafias, certainly Greek and Irish. There's even a Polish one: I have to admit it."

"What about an English Mafia?" Green asked.

"Ah, that's the only non-mafia in America. There's every hyphenated group you can think of: Serbo-American, Croat-American, Spanish-American. . . . They parade with flags and folk dances and everything, all except the English. The Irish march up Fifth Avenue cursing the English, but you never see the English marching up Fifth Avenue to curse the Irish. Of course, you know the reason." He was getting to his feet, after looking at his watch. "Sorry, I have to go. There's no English Mafia because the English just take it for granted they're superior; they were the first and they've stayed there. We all have to acknowledge it, don't we? We come to Scotland Yard, but not to the Sûreté, and certainly not to the Polish equivalent. Want to know what that's called?''

Green and Brougham had risen, too. "Spare us," Green said. "As a matter of fact," he added more seriously, "I happen to have a rather good relation with the Polish equivalent of the FBI on antiterrorism. They're very helpful and very agreeable. The ones I can't get on with are the Bulgarians. They're so peculiar that we can't enter into their minds. Did you hear about the defector they bumped off here by sticking his leg with a poisoned umbrella-point while he was just walking over Waterloo Bridge? Now I ask you. The Poles would never do that, would they? Far too sophisticated.''

Zeb was smiling broadly as he left. As far as he knew, he hadn't been able to help, but one could never tell, and at least Scotland Yard still had a pleasant mood to offer. "One day," he told Green as they walked to the front door together, "I must visit the Sherlock Holmes house in Baker Street. It is a museum, I suppose. My hero, Sherlock Holmes . . .''

Emilia had deliberately skipped the Friday meeting that Cranford had called. It was war now, and she decided to avoid a personal encounter before the news of her fortune came out and she had the weapon in her hands. Until then, she was up against a brick wall, what with the drive and power he exuded. She had to build up a base for herself, at speed. With this decision made, all was easy. She took five days of leave "for personal reasons," with no problem. Rhodine had rushed through her reports so that they could go without delay. Concorde was on the doorstep. By Friday evening they were in New York, installed in a suite at the Carlyle.

Joe Hogsheim and his wife, Patricia, had been waiting

for them at Kennedy, with a Rolls-Royce limousine in attendance. The art collection and a meeting with the trustees awaited them the next day in Philadelphia. In the meantime they were on the town. Emilia had thought of a quiet supper—say a lamb chop—and an early night. Rhodine had other ideas. She had told Rupert Mandeville that she was going to New York on Concorde and asked for an introduction or two, indicating that something not too dull would be welcome. They were barely in the Carlyle before the phone was ringing: Tim O'Leary, "friend of Roop." An hour later he had arrived, with only the mildest of invitations from Emilia, and was pouring the champagne that Hogsheim had had sent up. O'Leary was a stocky, pugnacious figure, heavily bearded and with a totally bald head, apparently shaven for effect. He had brought with him a very weird black girl called Sandra, immensely tall, sinuous, and beautiful, whom Rhodine recognized immediately as a famous model.

The press release with Emilia's name as the heiress was going to be out for the Sunday papers. Tim and Sandra were soon in the know, responding with whoops of excitement, and advice. "You want to keep out of the way overnight," Tim said, "otherwise some half-ass reporter's goin' to make a mess of the story. It's got to be a bombshell. We'll take you to the Village. What do you think, Sandra? Mama Lisa?"

"And then we can eat at the Burke. Yeah, that's just right. I can tell you one thing," Sandra said. "They'll love Rhodine at Mama Lisa's, but they'll just adore Emilia. Of course Rhodine is a chick, and they'll eat her up. I could eat her up myself. But wait till they see *you*, Emilia."

"Why me?" Emilia said, her colour rising.

" 'Cos you're special, that's why. They ain't seen

nothing like you before. You're real. That black outline. They never seen it. Really special."

Emilia felt very special just to hear this. What with Concorde and the Carlyle, New York was working. Was it the champagne? Cranford had disappeared from vision. Had he ever existed? There was Grandfather Wren, and now here she was herself, with this great black woman looking at her, and the Village ahead . . .

The Hogsheims bowed out once they had driven everybody downtown in the Rolls to Mama Lisa's crumbling old house at Tenth Avenue and Burke Street. The noise as they came into the huge black space hit them like a hurricane. With Sandra towering over the crowd, and Mama Lisa herself taking charge, they were soon at a large round table in what was clearly the choice room with a dozen other people attaching themselves in limpet style, the men with shirts open to the waist, the women like a flock of wildly coloured parakeets at the zoo.

Emilia, in her severe dark clothes was, it seemed, irresistible, the real thing. Everyone was after her. With one drink and then another, she was herself soon leading the way. Nothing had been said of her fortune, but with her look alone she stood out, symbolizing some kind of special English chic. It wasn't at all easy to see where she would end up. Afire in a very odd way, absorbing the dull thump of the music and the constant zoo noise of multilevel shouts and laughter, she had become a star in her own right, as if she'd popped out of Aston and Wren's like the cork of some vast Belshazzar of champagne. New York was pulsing through her in a spirit she had never dreamed of. In this mood the whole table, full of new fans, would be driving down to Philadelphia in the morning.

Rhodine, though upstaged as Sandra had predicted, watched it all with fascination and delight. It was a new Emilia, stepping up to the throne at Aston and Wren's, with Lord Cranford, all unknowing for the moment, about to be chopped down, surely, whenever she thought the moment had come. O'Leary, at Rhodine's side, had taken it all in with an intuitive grasp of the magic that had captured Emilia and what it might mean.

"Well, what do you know?" he murmured to Rhodine. "This isn't a bit like what Roop was telling me about your demure little lady-chum. I suppose when you suddenly inherit a fortune . . ."

"It's not just the money," Rhodine said. "You do know what's behind it all? She wants to take over at her business. She wants more than money for that. She's got to get rid of somebody first."

"Yeah, Roop was telling me. He said you were asking if I could find someone who could help her."

"Oh God, he didn't? I wasn't really serious. I was playing it like a movie script."

"Not what Roop said; he took it for real, all right. Very high stakes. Told me to think about it when I'd met her."

There was a sudden shout of laughter from across the table. Emilia had obviously said something which sounded outrageously funny, probably without knowing it. Perhaps she'd got the sexes mixed up in what seemed to them a delightfully innocent way. It was clear that she loved the applause that was suddenly coming her way, revelling in it, and sipping freely at the glass that was kept full.

Mama Lisa came up to enjoy the fun, all too ready to welcome a new star. Rhodine and O'Leary looked on for a moment.

"What about Roop's question?" he said to Rhodine. "I didn't take it too seriously, but now—well, she's quite a dame, isn't she? Might be fun to see how far she'll go."

Rhodine found herself laughing immoderately. "Oh, Tim. If you saw her in London! Shy isn't the word. Of course, there was more to it than that. I always felt there was something there ready to come out." She took a draft of her wine. "It's a question of willpower. I never really understood how much she had bottled up for when she would need it."

"I can see what you mean," O'Leary said, turning to greet a sardonic-looking man who had just sauntered over to join them. "Hi, Stogie. What do you think of my little English pet? Remember Roop when he was here? This is Rhodine—works in the same office."

"Hi, Rhodine," the man said. "Sure, I remember Roop. Quite a guy. Remember when he took on that black giant son of a bitch. Laid him out, too. Shouldn't have. Could have done himself an injury. He will if he comes back. Better tell him to keep away—Rhodine, is it?"

"Oh, I don't think anything fazes Roop," O'Leary drawled. "He knows what he's doing."

Rhodine had a sudden feeling that O'Leary was talking in code. This horrible man, Stogie, might be the kind of go-between O'Leary was thinking of. She shuddered to think of it. Was it just the flickering light and the thump of the music? One only caught sudden glimpses of a face or a couple of faces in a spotlight, without being able to decide if they were menacing or innocent. What of Stogie? No baby-faced monster from the movies. Better if he were, like Alan Ladd; one could accept that, but not this mean dark face. She looked across at Emilia, feeling protective. Hadn't they better move on? Sandra came over, ready to go, it seemed. They rescued Emilia. With shrieking farewells from her new fans, they were soon in a taxi being dropped a block away at a very different kind of place for dinner, Sandra welcomed by a svelte woman in charge called Rosa, with a table ready and celebrities being pointed out—the downtown "Heloise" they were told, with an implication that they should know what the uptown "Heloise" was famous for.

At least they could settle down here, with the sound of talk at a steady hum and no sardonic Stogie hovering over them as go-between to some dark deed or other. It was getting on for 2 or 3 A.M., London time. The elegance sustained them for a while, but it was a relief to be back at the Carlyle.

At nine next morning Joe Hogsheim was at the door with the Rolls. Two and a half hours later they were alighting in Philadelphia, with the trustees waiting at the museum—Emilia's museum—to show them the collection.

4

A WEEK AFTER STARTING some really solid work on the background she would need to draw on for the book, Vickie had gone to Oxford to have a long session on British industry with Beatrice Claire, a contemporary of hers as a student and now Fellow in Economic History at St. Anne's. Just talking to Bea might help her to identify the central questions. She had been preparing herself by reading standard works on the period and dipping into an assortment of official publications promising truly exciting reading, like the reports of the Macmillan Committee on Finance and Industry and the Radcliffe Committee papers on the Working of the Monetary System. What she was after was an indication in general terms of how Herbert Thomson, who swept the workshop floor as a teenager for five shillings a week, had managed to put his feet on the first rungs of the ladder. The key to what followed later surely lay in how he had conducted himself practically and psychologically—which included morally—in the early period. Once he was a few rungs up, expansion would have been easier; but how had it started, and in what form had it finally taken off?

Money—how did a poor boy get hold of cash at a time when British banks, as was increasingly clear, were universally unhelpful in financing small-business ventures? Dipping into Cranford's early papers and looking at some of the musty old newspaper cuttings that he had kept in haphazard form was enough to reveal the extraordinary gap between the old times and now. As far as she could see, no one in those days was rubbing industry's nose into the chances of profitable industry at home. No problem to assemble the shekels to finance a new tramcar system in Valparaiso; but factories at home had to make do with traditional business, keeping, as it were, to their own familiar tramlines. It had taken the rearmament dramas of the 1930s to shake things up; with the war over in 1945, the old pattern was back again until the merchant banks had taken off more recently both in direct expansion and wildcat amalgamations.

"I'm really curious about those who did get through," she said to Bea as they relaxed over tea. "I mean those whose names one doesn't read about in the papers. A little gossip would be a great help. I'm dining with Ambrose Usher tonight, and of course he's a master of gossip, but I have to know how to start him off."

Bea laughed. "Lucky you, dining with Ambrose. Bound to be fun. But I wouldn't expect him to know much about this. Now if you were researching something like Bosnian folklore in the sixteenth century, you couldn't find a better guide."

"Oh, I don't know. He seems to have rattled round in the modern world quite a lot. And he lived through those years in Washington when U.S. industry and finance were taking over everywhere. Wasn't it a front seat at the new industrial revolution? And he keeps going back on visits. No one knows why, but I suppose he has his old friends."

"Everyone thinks it's secret service," Bea said. "Spy stuff. After all, he was a contemporary of all the old Cambridge Bolshies. But that's over now, isn't it? They've all come out of the closet—both closets, so to speak."

"Do you think so?" Vickie said. "I've always thought that the Cambridge axis was too simple a concept. Oxford got off too easily. Not to mention other hot spots of the same disease, especially in Canada. Which reminds me. The U.S. expansion has been so revolutionary that it seems to dominate the earlier period too, but I keep getting odd hints in what I read that Canada has been written out of the story too readily. Today, of course, it's an appendage of the U.S. financially, but am I right to think that in the twenties and the thirties it was a lodestar for Britain in many ways now forgotten?''

"The Scottish connection was always very great," Bea said. "There's a lot to be written about Scottish enterprise in opening up Canada's west, and not just in oil and mining."

"I was thinking of it in more personal terms," Vickie said. "Some of the memoirs I've been reading seem to bring Canada very close as a kind of natural outlet for the British. It seems to have been a really special relationship. Of course Quebec upset this later on, but even there the British link was powerful. The last fling was the way they joined up to fight for England as soon as war was declared in 1939 . . ."

"And were furious when they got here and were told to sit still for a year during the Phony War."

"I suppose love-hate came into it," Vickie said. "Have you heard Oxford landladies on what Oxford had to put up with when the Canadians were stationed near here? They used to come into town to break things up at the weekend. They wanted a real war, with all the bloodletting of an ice-hockey game."

By coincidence Canada came up again, though in a different context, when Vickie was having a predinner drink with Ambrose in his rooms at St. Mary's. By this time, after a day of serious talk on the British economy, and with a pile of books from Bea for further reading, she was more than ready for light relief in the form of

Bosnian folklore or whatever form of frippery Ambrose might resort to. The pleasure seemed to be mutual.

"What a joy to see you," Ambrose said as she fell into an armchair. "I'm really stumped with what I was writing." He waved toward his desk, covered with a mass of assorted papers. "I feel close to what I want to say, but it isn't coming through clearly. Do you ever have that feeling?"

"Do I?" Vickie said. "All the time. But no one ever thinks *you* do. Beatrice Claire and I were gossiping about you only half an hour ago. She tells me that the view here is that your philosophy is just a cover and that your real interest is still the old spy stuff, which is why you keep going to Washington."

"Oh, good," Ambrose said. "I've been hoping that that's what people think. You see, it has one enormous advantage. If it's spies, no one can ask me what I'm working on, so I can carry on without being cross-examined all the time. Man of mystery: wonderful cover."

"And what *are* you working on?" Vickie asked. "Not cross-examination, just passionate interest. It seems pretty absorbing, to judge by your desk."

Ambrose had wandered over to a small table, ready to offer the drink. "Whisky and water," Vickie said. "Not too much water, I need to be restored. But don't forget my question. Now that you've come clean, I'm all agog."

"What am I working on?" He was muttering only half aloud as he handed Vickie the drink and took a sherry for himself. "Oh, dear, I feel a paradox coming on. If I give you a straight answer, it will be *ipso facto* a fib. However, you've asked for it. The straight answer is that I'm writing an essay on identity. But of course that's the same as working on spy stuff, which I said was just a cover. I suppose that's why I'm having such difficulty in putting it all on paper."

"Identity," Vickie murmured. "It covers everything, doesn't it? Including Cranford's life, if I really write the book."

"No," Ambrose said. "I'm pursuing something different. A biography expresses the unity of a character by bringing conflicting elements together. What I'm after is to see the individual as two conflicting elements which remain distinct."

"That's how you see a spy?"

"A spy is a good example, but the idea of double identity is wider than that. It's as if existence demands the ambivalence that all words project. The second half of the double defines the first half."

"Jekyll and Hyde?"

"Perfect. Each role is fulfilling. And not just with individuals. It can happen with adjacent countries, like England and Scotland, or the U.S. and Canada. I was thinking just now that Canada was one of the best examples. There's a virtually open border, so one can take on a double identity, passing back and forth, without deceit and without losing the validity of each role. The identity of every Canadian, however patriotic, is defined by the presence of the U.S.A. within his psyche. If I were writing a thriller, I'd make that the heart of the mystery."

"Double identity." Vickie was clearly very taken with the concept. "Yes, very pervasive. It's always supposed to be the answer to the riddle in that famous story by Joseph Conrad in which the young captain shelters a murderer who is really his other self."

"Yes, *The Secret Sharer*. I've brought that in," Ambrose said. "A fiction writer must always feel the double identity very clearly. All fiction is a spy story, in which the author is leading a double life. Sometimes he takes a pseudonym to express it, but he doesn't need to. That's why it's both right and wrong to expect fiction to be the *real* life of the author. It's the *other* life. I came across a delightful story about Jorge Luis Borges which illustrates this perfectly. Someone sees him in the street and says, "You're Borges, aren't you?" And he replies: "At times."

"Oh, that's very nice. But he's a special case, isn't he? As an artist he was on the lookout for different identities, and he was completely at home in English literature, and probably French, so he had a head start."

"But it's equally true of all immigrants," Ambrose said. "After all, I should know: the eternal alien completely at home. America's the prime example—'a land of orphans' someone called it, a land of doubles. Everyone there's got a hyphen in them, like a Maréchal's *baton* with a Frenchman. I gather your Lord Cranford hasn't got a hyphen anywhere, which should make it easier for you. He's a thousand percent English?"

"More than that," Vickie said. "A thousand percent Yorkshire. No double identities there. I believe that every U.S. state has an individual identity like that. Were you pursuing this in America when you were there?"

"Only incidentally," Ambrose said. "I came across one truly American manifestation of the subject through a friend at the Massachusetts Institute of Technology. You know Americans believe that intuition, which we rather rely on, never takes you as far as a mechanical process. They showed me a huge computer they've developed at M.I.T. which puts all examples of American identity at one's disposal through being fed with a fantastic variety of information about the U.S. population. It covers origins, names, speech styles, professions, and family connections, and that establishes extraordinary links not just of today, but going back. They call it a psychofingerprint computer, with the content changing automatically all the time."

"Like the supplements to the *New Oxford Diction-*

ary," Vickie said. "New words, new pronunciations, new connections are recorded the moment anyone's aware of them, instead of a hundred year later, as they used to be."

"One day all these computers will be writing the books for you."

"My God, I wish they would," Vickie said, and immediately added: "No, I don't. I want to find things out myself, on the ground, so to speak. I'm going up to Yorkshire next week, as it happens, to try and talk to people who knew industry there in the 1920s and thirties. I want to get the atmosphere right."

"Cranford doesn't help?"

"Yes. He offered every kind of help. I'm going up to their Suffolk home, in fact, this weekend." Oddly enough, she felt reluctant to go further in talking of Cranford's own early experiences. It might be breaking the agreement in which everything in this field had to be kept personal to the two of them. When Ambrose had talked of double influences, she had thought of the conflict Cranford had spelt out between the Old Testament and the New in his childhood, and the heritage it seemed to have left. Was this just with him, or was it part of the northern world at large? Was Cranford ultimately just a blunt Yorkshireman, like a character in a J. B. Priestley novel? Surely no one was as simple and blunt as that.

She had been listening too much to Ambrose, she decided; a basketful of complexity all rolled into one. Still he did stir one up with his talk of double identity. She would start using this as a key for her private assessment of acquaintances old and new. How would Laurence have fared, now a double identity himself in distant Brisbane? Serve him right. And what about Felix Morgan, a ready-made double more closely at hand? She was seeing him in a couple of days, before going to

77

Yorkshire. What bombs might he defuse for her in one way or another?

Odd how being at Oxford for a day gave one a great sense of distance from the workaday world while at the same time burying one within its various immediacies. Joining the Fellows in the Senior Common Room for the ritual sherry before trooping into Hall for dinner under Ambrose's courteous guidance, she had first been given an extremely warm welcome, *more academico,* as the author of a prize-winning book, but within a minute had found herself being criticized—almost sneered at—by a South African, introduced as the chemistry Fellow, who seemed to take strong exception to the sympathy she had shown in her book for, as he put it, that "reactionary proto-Fascist Kruger," in whose memory the Transvaal had now gone over openly to Hitlerite racial doctrines under a deliberately Nazi-style flag. Ambrose, rescuing her rather swiftly, saw to it that she was seated at the High Table with a gentle art historian called Neville Harrow on her right. But even this took one back firmly into quasi-political argument. The newspapers and television since the previous Sunday had been carrying quite a few stories of Miss Emilia Marritt inheriting the priceless paintings of her Philadelphia uncle, with an indication that they were now to be sold and dispersed. Wasn't this a great scandal, Mr. Harrow said to her, typical of the anticultural attitude of the present government. As an Oxford woman herself, would she not join the committee now being set up to have the whole collection bought for Oxford and installed at the Examination Schools, a more than handsome setting, with a constant audience of students and visitors who would be enriched by their presence? He had had an idea on this, he told her. Miss Marritt apparently worked at the London publishers Aston and Wren, whose chairman had just escaped from a bomb assault. As an act of gratitude, could he not buy the collection for Oxford through the cooperation of Miss Marritt, a member of his company? Surely the heiress would be agreeable under these circumstances. How did one approach Lord Cranford to push this idea forward?

"A charming idea," Ambrose told him, leaning across Vickie to take part in the discussion. "You have chosen the right messenger to pursue this idea. A hit, a palpable hit."

Vickie looked at him, grateful for his not taking it further. If, as Ambrose pretended, it was a charming idea, it was not one likely to interest the Lord Cranford she knew. However, she had not met the heiress. Maybe she was closely attached to Cranford and would be happy to pursue this idea with him as a symbol of their friendship. One never knew.

In the train back to London, Vickie could still luxuriate for a time in the other-worldly atmosphere that was, in the end, the real hallmark of Oxford. At some point—was it at Paddington Station?—one came back for the crossing-point, or the bridging-point, between it and the different time-scales or value-scales of the ordinary world. Ambrose, in his talk of double identity, had seen the need, in a biography, to bring all conflicts together. Would she achieve this in her book? In the last chapter, perhaps. In the meantime one had to let events take their course, hoping for something quite unexpected to be the solvent.

A writer was not the only one who looked for change this way. For Emilia Marritt, the unexpected transformation had started through the first visit to America. She had let go in a wholly different world, and had found America taking hold of her life in ways that even she was not yet fully aware of.

In her own mind she had worked out that after the return to England she would pursue a rational programme that would lead her straight to the chairmanship. But Rhodine was a wild card in the hand, with Emilia quite incapable of working out the implications. It hadn't seemed so at the beginning. Rhodine was everything to her, in a nice English way. But New York was neither nice nor English, which could play hell with someone who, like Rhodine, was prepared to follow New York wherever it led.

Emilia had herself responded this way on her first arrival, but for the most part had kept an even course once the heiress business got into its stride. The publicity that thrust itself forward when the news broke might have diverted her had not Joe Hogsheim advised, for good legal reasons, to play things quietly for the moment. All TV and interview requests were, in his view, to be turned down. The museum people, he said, had still to be nursed along to accept the situation with good will, and a careless word in publicity—say about her uncle's quarrel with them—might get things on the wrong track. They had been grudgingly pleased to accept four paintings as offered by Emilia, and were marshalling support to buy others at the sale. Their real annoyance had risen over Rhodine's choice for herself of a small Mary Cassatt head of a girl, but they would no doubt get over it in time.

Emilia, having accepted Hogsheim's advice on curtailing publicity, had been anxious to get back to London as fast as she could to pursue the other plans in her mind. In the event, they had gone back from Philadelphia to New York on the Monday and booked to take Concorde to London on the following day. She had agreed with Hogsheim to return in three or four weeks, when she would allow herself time to undertake all the practical things connected with the Sotheby sale.

The most difficult factor in taking a cool decision in the American atmosphere had proved to be Rhodine, who was happily exploring a special kind of New York lifestyle opening up to her under the tutelage of Tim O'Leary and his friend, the sinister-looking Stogie. Emilia herself, recalling the excitement that had surfaced so positively for her at Mama Lisa's, had found it not quite the same when they had settled down on Monday evening at Heloise Uptown, where everything seemed tailored to *chic* rather than outrage. The word had got round, of course, and some people did come up to inspect the heiress and offer congratulations. She was less responsive, because her mind was already halfway back to London, ready for the battle that was to face her in the formal atmosphere of a board meeting at Aston's.

For Rhodine, in contrast, the New York she was now seeing was totally absorbing. The advertising world at home was lively enough, with Roop's freewheeling nonchalance adding its own flavour; but there was nothing in the underground reaches of Clapham or Notting Hill to match the spirit of sky's-the-limit and no-holds-barred that seemed to be taken for granted among the people she was now meeting. On their last night in New York, Sandra, huge and sinuous, had attached herself to Rhodine and now proposed to take them on to a joint in Harlem unavailable to ordinary visitors. Emilia said she was too tired and went back to the Carlyle. Rhodine went off with Sandra and some of the others, racing through the litter-strewn streets to an obscure hideaway that seemed dangerous enough just in its setting, with men lounging around—obvious guards—outside the barred doorways. She could not have said coherently, when she got back to the hotel around six in the morning, what had gone on in music and other things. She did remember, faintly, talking to O'Leary at one point about Emilia's pressing need to push Lord Cranford out of the way, and how it had nearly happened in the most convenient way through the IRA bomb. O'Leary, when he heard this, had exchanged a peculiar look with Stogie. "Sounds like a job for Billie," he had muttered, with Stogie nodding in accord. But this was only a split second in her memory of the evening.

Roop added a gloss to this a few days later in London when she told him about her New York adventures as they sat drinking at the Dog and Duck. He smiled broadly when she recalled, without much assurance, hearing the mention of Billie. "Your surprises are just beginning," he said. "Little Rhodine is growing up." "What's it all about?" she asked him, but he just went on smiling.

In the meantime Emilia had begun a growing-up of a different kind, seeming to sense for the first time the feeling of power that had arrived with money, and getting ready to exploit it in any way she could. The messages of congratulation at her good fortune had piled up in the office to greet her return, and most significant for the future seemed the reaction from Cranford himself. She had phoned Aston's from New York to say that she would be in the office on Wednesday, but Felix Morgan, thinking for himself, had telephoned her at home late on Tuesday. "Absolutely marvellous," he had said. "The boss wants to talk to you the moment you're in. He wants to know everything. He particularly wants to be sure you'll come to a meeting set for Friday at eleven. He's brought forward the proposal you made last week when you talked to him. Of course I want to know everything, too, and I have more time than he has. I'll pop in to see you tomorrow some time."

By itself, the reaction from Cranford sounded promising. In this mood, and with her new feeling of self-confidence, she could surely manoeuvre him into giving up the chairmanship. Money did talk, it seemed. She had

82

the same feeling when she had a brief word with Cranford on the phone after she came in on Wednesday. "I expect you've had lots of new ideas now," he said to her, which she took to mean that he would, after all, be encouraging her plans.

"Lots of new ideas," she responded in the same spirit, leaving talk of her particular series on one side for the moment.

It was important, it seemed to her, to use the intervening time to test the attitude of her co-directors, in case the issue actually came to a head at the meeting. Discussing her strategy in advance with Rhodine, she had accepted the idea that she should invite the directors and the other senior editors to a celebratory glass of champagne at five in the afternoon. Felix Morgan had said that Cranford—and he himself—would not be free at this time because of a meeting at Cranford's office in the UEI building. This suited her. The others were all too happy to accept. The new Emilia was learning not to skimp. The chairman-to-be was to show how she would play the role. Champagne from the Covent Garden Wineshop— on use or return—was to be as free as tap water, with ice and glasses, and a wine-waiter standing by. There is no office that doesn't respond to this kind of festivity, especially if it takes place without a preliminary whip-round. The flow of good nature, and even affection, mounted to the popping of corks. Emilia herself sipped abstemiously from one glass, aware, perhaps unconsciously, that she had to appear more authoritative than frolicsome. The Mama Lisa performance belonged elsewhere and was long over.

With one exception, the colleagues she had spoken to during the day seemed to be responding to the feeling she was trying to generate by talking of how good it felt to have had this marvellous luck while still at Aston's. Some picked up the idea perfectly. Leo Forrest, specialist in science and nature books—always very expensive to produce—held up his glass to her for a direct kind of toast. "All that lovely money," he said. "Just hand it all over and we'll produce the most marvellous illustrated books. We'll corner the market. How about it, Emilia?" Josephine Trout was equally responsive, though in a different way. "I've been meaning to ask you," she said, "if you'll support me with an idea I have for a new series of political books like *Evil in the North,* issue them like the Left Book Club in the thirties, not exactly paperback but sort of very identifiable, not yellow like the Gollancz books but perhaps a terrific scarlet colour that I've discovered, bring them out two a month, strong political line, sell very cheap, of course they'll cost a lot more, but they'll be pro-American so Lord Cranford should approve. Do you think he'll put up the money? There's that reserve fund he insisted on and that you've been looking after, haven't you? Well now, you're a whiz on money matters yourself."

A possible ally, Emilia thought as the Trout wandered on. They were all potentially useful, all, that is, except for Warren Faversham. Something was different about him. He had always been very satirical about Cranford, leading off in the joke-making about our little Herbie, but today, though making free with the champagne, he seemed strangely subdued, even worried. What was the matter? she wondered. He had joked with her in the past about Grandfather Wren, and how she ought to be the natural heir to the first-floor office, but now, though he did say something about being an heiress on two fronts, there was a certain bitterness about it. "You can take off in any direction now," he said, though he well knew that all her loyalty was to Aston and Wren, without the slightest desire to take off anywhere else. Had she offended him in some way, perhaps by not talking to him first about the women's book series? Or was it envy, pure and simple? She couldn't count on him at the meeting, she felt. Something was wrong.

And so indeed it proved at the board meeting on Friday. In a few days she had become a minor celebrity in England, and Cranford said something about it as they gathered round the table. He picked it up again after they had disposed of routine matters and had turned to "Other Business." In the friendliest way, he asked Emilia if she would like to talk of the series she had proposed to him.

She had come to the meeting armed with a good preliminary list of the books she had in mind, with titles and editors, and a broad picture of the running costs and potential sales. Surely all was well. She was well briefed and seemed to be floating on a cloud of friendship from Cranford himself, far different from the hostility he had expressed at the earlier meeting. But as she began to speak, the old feeling came back. Cranford was sitting there with a faint smile on his face, biding his time. The company was his, and no one was going to foist old-fashioned books, full of mawkish feminism, on him. Obviously, he still exuded the kind of power that left no one else a chance to get in.

Briefly he went round the table for comment, and it was as if they knew. Leo Forrest was good-natured about it, but not enthusiastic. Josephine Trout asked if they could consider an alternative proposal for a series that would be up-to-date, dealing with current political questions. Faversham went further. For no reason she could think of he led the talk into a kind of eulogy for Cranford, suggesting that they should draw on his business sense and knowledge of the world to produce a type of book that would portray Britain's real role in history. Emilia listened in amazement. Faversham seemed almost to be toadying Cranford, who clearly enjoyed hearing the things he had said in public speeches coming back from the company's senior director.

"Well, we must think about Emilia's proposal," Cranford said, bringing the meeting to a close. She had lost, and would always lose against this kind of psychological power. Her serious proposal had only been a test of strength, but it showed what was to happen. The full story was that nothing would ever move him except of his own volition, and even if these faint-hearted colleagues might be ready one day to welcome her as chairman, they certainly would do nothing to get him out of the way.

"We must think about it," he had said. Yes: think about it and find new ways to make it work. She would talk about it to Rhodine, and see what she thought.

Emilia had been quite right to detect a peculiar change in Faversham's attitude, though she could never have guessed that his depression was linked to a meeting the day before with the owner of a rather jolly antique shop in Suffolk. George Sekelis had come to town for an exhibition of needlepoint at the Victoria and Albert Museum. They had met there after lunch by arrangement, the latest stage in a feeling of danger that was now obsessing Faversham.

At lunch that day, the danger, though very real to him, had been softened by the comforting atmosphere of Brooks's. His guest, a young Harvard historian called Sebastian Goldberg, was engaged in a major book on England's left-wing movements in the thirties, and had found his way to Aston's through Faversham's alert determination to discover what might come out in a book of this kind.

Goldberg certainly seemed to know his way around the subject. He had done a highly acclaimed book for Knopf, in New York, on the trade union leader John L.

Lewis, and it was a friend at Knopf who had tipped off Faversham about the new project. There was no knowing what a gifted researcher might turn up about elements in the 1930s story that were still buried. Faversham's own involvement had thrown up only the faintest of rumours so far, but if any associate showed signs of talking now, with names and places listed, it could spell trouble, as George Sekelis had reminded him so painfully. It was a lucky chance that young Goldberg had become available. If there was a hint en route that Faversham's own story was going to blow, the ultimate—the flight—might be called for. Any advance warning could be precious.

One couldn't just rely on getting hold of the Masterson revelations from Cranford's archives before he used them. There were others like Masterson who had wavered for a time with appeals to what had been the zeitgeist, but finally let things come out. Getting into Cranford's house was certainly the top priority: one couldn't leave a time-bomb ticking away forever. But if there was a hint of other leads, they always had to be followed up.

What Faversham had to determine over lunch was whether Goldberg's own background had thrown up leads that might be decisive. Growing up in Hollywood as the son of a major movie producer, he must certainly have been given a thorough education in the varieties of Russian attachments that had surfaced there, ranging from parlour-pink innocents through more decisive activists and moving ultimately into the realm of those who took orders and executed them as part of the machine. Faversham had fallen into this realm for a while at an early stage, and had spent the last ten years hoping that nothing would now come out. If Goldberg was aware of this, even partially, his demeanour at lunch was masterly. He knew every name, was full of questions, but gave no sign that Faversham's involvement had left any trace that was now relevant. Faversham formed the view that Goldberg probably saw him as a parlour innocent, with a foot among all the old comrades, never fully committed, but interested and helpful, the perfect publisher, therefore, for this kind of book.

Giles Corby, who really fitted this profile, came up to the table while they were lunching, with a slight indication to Faversham that he was looking for a private word later. Goldberg knew Corby's name as the author of *English Country Houses*; not surprisingly, given his special interest, he also knew that the two men had been at Cambridge together. There was a little twinkle in Corby's eye when he heard Goldberg say this, and the reason became clear when he and Faversham had their private word, emerging from the men's room. "It's very funny," he said to Faversham. "Do you remember my telling you that the Immigration people held me up on my last trip to the U.S.A.? Well, it goes on. At a party at the U.S. Embassy a couple of days ago, a chap there—I'm sure he was in Intelligence, he looked so stupid—was talking about my book and just happened to ask if you had published it. Weren't you at Cambridge together? he asked me. And now here's your friend Mr. Goldberg on the same tack. They really have gone crazy about Cambridge since the Blunt business. I thought I'd better tell you."

Goldberg joined them as they walked to the door and exchanged farewells. Faversham was adding things up. He had not really decided how to evaluate Goldberg's position in this field, but it was certainly good that he had established some sort of rapport with him, at a time when things seemed to be coming out. All in all, it looked as if the Masterson report, or whatever it was, might be the decisive factor. If Cranford came across it among all the other papers, would he himself be able to evaluate what Masterson had written, or would he hand it all to a researcher or MI5? Sekelis might have some clue by now, though one never really knew how to treat Sekelis with his odd interests, first cricket and now needlepoint. In a way his oddity was itself very English, unregimented, very personal. If one could get rid of the nightmare, one could actually enjoy him.

Waving goodbye to Goldberg, whom he was now calling Sebastian, Faversham stood for a moment on the steps of Brooks's, watching the lovely black taxis chasing each other up St.James's Street toward Piccadilly. How beautiful London was on a May day like this. Mrs. Thatcher had been complaining that London was untidy and a disgrace. Perhaps it was, in *her* milieu, but not in St. James's Street, where everything was classic in the English way, without anyone having designed it, the men in their bowler hats, the women colourful and fashionable in an offbeat kind of way, the buildings higgledy-piggledy but agreeable to look at, a palace at the foot of the hill; Brown's Hotel, which no one could have designed, a stone's throw away in the opposite direction.

How awful, how unbearable it would be if he had to run off and give this all up because of some unredeemed actions of the past. Philby had had to flee because he was still in the middle of things, but *he* had long forgotten them. To go on living in England but disgraced, as Blunt had done, would be impossible for him. Yet Cranford would surely feel he had to denounce him if Faversham's name was in Masterson.

A raised hand brought a taxi to him quietly and with perfect courtesy. At the V. and A., with Sekelis waiting, the sense of happiness vanished. A second look-around Pelham Court by Sekelis's agent in the guise of a gas man had not been fruitful, and Pierre had decided that they would try more seriously during the festival, working their way in during the other distractions. How could Sekelis be so casual about it? He really seemed more concerned about the outcome of the festival cricket match against Lazenby. Faversham must come, he insisted. The village green was a delightful setting, and their chances of a win were improving. It was true that a man who worked at the Lazenby garage had emerged this season as an excellent bat, but Ashenham in turn had discovered a demon bowler, only sixteen but fantastically good.

Back at Aston's, Faversham felt increasingly depressed. He did his best to be polite during the champagne party that Emilia Marritt had set up to celebrate her great inheritance, but the whole thing was so absurd and transparent that he could hardly bring himself to smile. She was obviously aiming to try and buy Cranford out, now that she had all this money. Could anything be more ridiculous? Cranford had more power in one minute of his presence than Marritt could produce in a thousand years. One had to admire power even if, at the same time, one feared it. To his own surprise, he found himself speaking up for Cranford at the directors' meeting. Yet what chance was there that Cranford would fail to act if the story was revealed to him in the Masterson document? No motivation would make it possible. Pierre and Sekelis were right. They would have to take action.

5

THE DAY FOR VICKIE'S visit to Pelham Court had come at last. She knew that it would be a Stately Home, with all that was implied, but nothing had prepared her for the haphazard but wonderfully spacious beauty of the setting. This was how to judge wealth, she decided: not in terms of the oppression of the poor old villeins of Norman times who had wrested it out of the virgin woodlands, or the Yorkshire factory hands of our own days whose labours had provided Herbert Thomson with the money to buy it all. Only the end product mattered when something like this emerged through nature, or history, or the English genius for combining grandeur with intimacy.

A vast curving drive opened up repeatedly into entrancing tree-clusters, hillocks, and ponds. The house itself was a mediaeval court on a very grand scale, with a scattering of lodges and cottages, coach-houses and stables, turrets and follies folded into the landscape, the timber, plaster, stone, and brick speaking in various tongues but always in friendship. In the distance, across a stretch of trees, one saw the Barn emerging, the huge roof leading the eye on endlessly with its promise of plenty in a biblical mode, a barn flowing with corn and wine and cattle. In two weeks it would flow with art and music and theatre to bring out a new kind of promise. Vickie stood marvelling at it all. The work that lay ahead in doing the book was already recompensed for her in having been brought here.

Felix Morgan had given no sign of equal wonder when she had dined with him at La Turquoise the night before. He had conceded that it was "quite a place," but that could mean anything. Perhaps it was small compared to vast establishments he may have seen in Wyoming or Texas. Americans normally loved English country houses however small, but maybe this one wasn't enough of a gem. They also liked some distinctive literary flavour, linked to Jane Austen or the Brontës, which Pelham didn't proclaim.

Truth to tell, his main interest was personal, and in a very agreeable way. "Call me Felix," he had said, obviously very determined to be friends. "How are you getting on with the book? Tell me everything." He seemed to have a deeper interest than just to hear about the book, and she liked the way it came out. He was terribly good looking, his fair hair rather tousled, his eyes alight with humour and intelligence. "What I wait for," he said, "is to see how you assess the boss psychologically. I know him pretty well and yet in a way I don't, especially about his early background. I'm longing to hear how it all got going. I suppose you may find interviews and magazine articles precisely on that. Could be very interesting."

"I'll be trying for something personal like that," she said. "I'm going up to Yorkshire next week to build things up from there, on precisely the early years and all that. I won't be writing it up for a long time, of course, but I hope to get the feeling."

"You must tell me all about it," he said. "At least as much as you can."

Vickie remembered the barriers imposed on this. She'd have to watch her step a bit, but surely there was an area for exchanging background talk. "I'll be trying to see who's still there from his old associates," she said. "His first wife died, didn't she? But I suppose her family might still have some survivors who'll talk. I'm looking forward to meeting his present wife when I go to Pelham Court tomorrow.''

"Margaretta is wonderful," he said. "Terrifically good looking, in a kind of dark Italian style. And she's highly intelligent."

"Is she a good actress?"

"I've only seen her in what we call off-Broadway shows, with short runs. She only works part-time, but she's very keen. I wouldn't say she's the greatest, but she does present herself very well. I thought it was very interesting that she managed to persuade the boss to let her do the show she's putting on at the festival, scenes from a rather off-beat French novel called *Dangerous Liaisons*, which I expect you know."

"Yes, Lord Cranford told me," Vickie said. "I was rather surprised. I thought it was rather way-out for a barn performance in deepest Suffolk. It must appeal to her in some special way. Perhaps she identifies with it."

"That must be it, I suppose," Felix said. "It must be a strange experience being an actress—or an actor. One becomes somebody else, but maybe that other person is already there."

"A double identity?" Vickie said. "Yes, I was talking about this to a philosopher friend at Oxford just this week. He thought that all kinds of people can have a double identity like that. It's acceptable on the stage, but it would be very disconcerting if it affected the characters one met in ordinary life."

"Yet it can happen," Felix said. "Maybe it's not as disturbing as it sounds. It could add another dimension to life, a sense of freedom perhaps."

Vickie shuddered a little. "I don't think I really like it. I think I'm more prosaic as a biographer. It's probably a limitation. I'm not enough of a psychologist, or fantasist."

It was a feeling that had stayed with her after she got home from dinner. Was her whole approach to writing too matter-of-fact? The thought came back next day when she got out of her beloved old Ford Capri and stood looking at Pelham Court, turning in one direction and another to try to absorb the subtleties and satisfactions of the view. Coming to a place like this was part of the act of transformation that she felt growing around her. It had started, in a way, by hearing about the bomb in the BBC news bulletin, which was like the tympanum that precedes the raising of the curtain in a French theatre. So much had come on the stage: Cranford with his talk of crime and punishment, Felix Morgan opening up life for her in a different way. A new dimension, he had said. She felt that herself, thinking of him. A new freedom . . .

The butler had seen her drive up, and opened the door. Behind him, Lady Cranford came out in greeting. "So glad you could come," she said to Vickie. "Herbert had told me how much he enjoyed meeting you."

"It was mutual. We had a wonderful talk."

"You'll find him more relaxed here. He simply loves it. I, too. We were so lucky to get it when Lord Tenderden died. Really endless pleasure."

She looked to be around forty and was, as Felix had said, strikingly beautiful in a dark Italian style. Her voice was well modulated, with an American accent that seemed to have lost any regional origin. The actress had taken over in the way she spoke and moved.

"Herbert will be out soon," she said. "He gets absorbed in his papers even down here. Would you like me to show you around a little?"

Totally gracious. For a split second Vickie saw it as a performance, Ruth Draper showing off a few family pictures—a Rembrandt or two—that they happened to have around. What was she really like? Surely not as smooth as this. Or do actresses always give performances?

The salon they moved into was full of treasures. A large picture on one wall looked like a Breughel. A Chinese screen nearby also had an entrancing snow scene. Vickie exclaimed in wonder. Drinks were waiting on the terrace outside.

"We took it all over as it stood from Lord Tenderden," Lady Cranford said. "There are masses more paintings in a kind of storeroom, a huge variety of things that his ancestors collected on trips to Europe. And there were lots of manuscripts and papers. Herbert is particularly interested in the papers. Lord Tenderden was so old when he died that most of these papers are unclassified. Herbert works on them every weekend; he wants to go through them all before he decides what library to present them to. It will take him a long time to sort them out, but he wants to do it all himself, though I suppose he may ask you to help him, of course. I really don't know. It's all very personal with him."

"I know the feeling," Vickie said. "But just now you must all be very busy with the festival preparations. I hope I can see this famous barn after lunch."

"Absolutely. It's immensely long and beautiful. I'm doing a play there, or scenes from a play."

"Yes," Vickie said. "Lord Cranford told me. *Les Liaisons Dangereuses*. It sounds fascinating."

"I've got an excellent actor working with me on it. You'll meet him in a few minutes: Patrick Hearn. He's staying for the weekend; very Irish, very elegant, in a style of Alan Badel. Did you like Badel's work?"

"Oh, very much. Very distinctive."

"We're going to do some rehearsing after lunch in one of the stables, which is fine for rehearsing. We'll clear off and that will leave you time to have a long talk with Herbert. Ah, here's Patrick now."

He was indeed elegant—tall and with a rich brogue that was like music. "We're setting the play in Ireland," Lady Cranford said. "Early twentieth century, with the Anglo-Irish in full swing, much more convincing here than a French setting."

"Much more rotten," Patrick Hearn said. "Every word of villainy rings true."

The Anglo-Irish setting sounded very imaginative, Vickie thought. Most original. And she liked Hearn's obvious enjoyment of the idea of carefree villainy. The two of them seemed to have fallen happily into the roles, matched perfectly in looks as the Marquise and the Viscount, and with an obviously strong personal rapport.

"Patrick's coaching me in the accent," Lady Cranford said.

"She's very good," he said. "Much better than I was in an American play we've just done in Glasgow, where I was supposed to be an Italian Mafia type. Margaretta coached *me* on that, but I don't think it rang true."

"He was trying to imitate Marlon Brando in *The Godfather*," Margaretta exclaimed. "No one can get away with that."

They were laughing happily as Lord Cranford came in. He was very welcoming, and lunch was pleasant enough. But the atmosphere had changed. One would have said that Cranford's mind was elsewhere, brooding about something. It came out later when Margaretta and Patrick went off to rehearse, and Vickie sat down for a talk with her host on the terrace.

At first, Cranford talked, as Vickie hoped he would, about early days in Yorkshire. She had decided not to involve him at this stage in her plan to go there two days later, picking up the traces for herself. When she had got a feeling about the place, she could ask a few leading questions to take things further; but for the moment all she wanted from Cranford was to hear him talk spontaneously and without cross-examination.

As he began to talk she soon realised that it was not going to be easy to put colour or excitement into the story of poverty and sobriety that was now confirmed. If the psychoanalytic approach had been her style—which it wasn't—she would no doubt have looked for the key to his own drive in the fact that he was an only child, his mother constantly ill and haggard after his birth, and dying when he was sixteen. Was it equally significant that Father was equally drab? Chapel was the only passion. What a misery, Vickie thought.

It was when he came to talk of Baxby and Thomson, the first independent company in which he began to mount the ladder, that a certain liveliness came into the story. He was twenty-two when he first met Joe Baxby, who owned and ran a small engineering repair shop in a South Yorkshire town called Shilton. He was vague on the earlier jobs—obviously very humble ones—after leaving school, but grew lively in describing how he had persuaded Joe Baxby to take him on at five pounds a week, a princely wage. "You see, I'd developed a way of getting all kinds of metal-cutting processes handled automatically in a revolutionary way to replace everything done by hand at enormous cost in time and manpower. I'd taken out quite a lot of patents on this. It was just before rearmament, and the whole thing mushroomed. It was all through my patents and initiative. At the end of the first year, the company became Baxby and Thomson. By 1940 we had five thousand people in ten factories in different parts of England and Scotland. After Dunkirk, output grew ten times, and the government sent me to the U.S.A. to amalgamate with some American companies who had the capacity to expand on an enormous scale with us."

He grew rather misty-eyed recalling the mergers. "The

American ones were the most significant. One big development in the late 1950s was when we took on a big involvement, with cash and share exchanges, in a huge engineering corporation in Ohio called Mercantile Universal Products—M.U.P. You'll see a lot about that in my papers. Not everything appears on paper, of course. A lot of this kind of dealing is person to person, but I'll help you in explaining things. M.U.P. has close connections with some influential Italian people and corporations. I think you know what I mean. The Mafia has infiltrated a lot. Some people might have sniffed at our keeping these close links, but it didn't bother me. Why should it? Our business is honest enough, and if some Mafia people decide to invest their cash into business instead of laundering it through the Cayman Islands or Antigua, why not? Many of these corporation chiefs became good friends of mine, especially Fred Masolino. I believe he's run into trouble recently with a grand jury investigation, but it doesn't worry me at all. It's routine over there."

"It's interesting how involved you are with America. You like their way of doing business?"

Cranford leaned forward excitedly. "It's like a breath of fresh air compared with the stuffy processes over here. Of course England is the greatest country for me in a personal sense. I'm very patriotic, and they gave me this title. But I've spent a great deal of my working time over there and enjoyed every minute of it. I've tried to import much of it here. Felix Morgan is a good case. Fred Masolino offered him to me, and I think he's good. And of course there's one other prize . . ." He broke off smiling.

"You mean your wife?"

"Margaretta. That's just what I do mean. Where would you find an English woman like that? I met her, in fact, at a party given by Fred. Her family's Italian, lovely

98

name—Paradiso. My first wife, Helen, had died five years earlier, and I'd been very lonely. Of course Margaretta's very much younger than I am. She would have a different kind of relationship with a younger man. I think you know what I mean. But she's immensely stimulating, partly through her stage interests. Not that I always understand what she's after in this."

"Like the play they're doing at the festival?"

Cranford paused for a minute. It was clear that talk of the play had reawakened some trouble in his mind. "Yes," he said finally. "We talked about this the other day. I told you that I agreed to her putting it on because it's got a moral ending. Those two wicked people are punished at the end, as they should be. But I still don't like what goes on in the play before they're punished. It's very cynical, really immoral, but I don't see what I can do now. Margaretta insists that it's very high quality in literary terms, very elegant, she keeps saying. But I can't see why we should have to admire anything that's cynical when there are so many good things one could write about. I'm not at all sure that I like seeing her expressing all those wicked ideas. I probably won't go to the actual performance. I want to spend as much time as I can working on some papers here that I've got involved in. It's something I want to talk to you about. In a way, it relates to the play, or at least to crime and punishment. I think I can tell you about it, without revealing any secrets, just so that you can see the way my mind's been working on this."

He paused again. Obviously what he had to say was immensely important to him. He seemed to have been wrestling with some deep moral problem that had now resolved itself. Vickie had become a kind of confessor, and he needed to talk.

"I told you the other day," he said, "that I want to see how my life adds up morally. I'm ready to face evil acts that I've done, at least I *think* I am. I believe that when something evil has been done, the sinner has to accept punishment. The world is built on this principle. It may not be punishment in a court. It could be punishment by self-recognition. I was very clear about all this, as you know. Well, something has happened to me now that makes me doubt this. I'll tell you."

He had been sitting huddled up with concentration; but now he shifted and seemed to be more at ease with himself.

"When I bought this house, it came with all the contents, though I agreed with the trustees to hand on any papers that were not, so to speak, art objects, books, and so on that could go into a sale. I had one thing in mind particularly. When I spoke to Lord Tenderden shortly before his death, he told me that he'd been trying for years to get to the bottom of all the treachery that had affected the British upper classes. He seemed to feel that spying for Russia was a kind of personal insult to him. There were still some people who had not yet been formally charged, and he was trying to get evidence that would get this done. I think it was mixed up with a kind of personal vendetta that he had against the government. It would be a way of getting even with them. But the deepest thing was to expose the traitors. He told me, under every kind of oath of secrecy, that a man of his acquaintance, who had himself been one of these Communist traitors, had put down everything he knew in a detailed report, with names and other details, going back for thirty years, and had handed it to him. Lord Tenderden was checking it all very discreetly before bringing it out as a bombshell attack on the government. And in the middle of all this he had a sudden stroke and died. I was able to buy the house and all contents, which include a great mass of papers which I've got locked up in my office with total security. I've been going through the papers at weekends, delaying any handover I may have to do. As you can imagine, I wanted to find this report if it existed, and to take a decision on what I should do with it. Well, I've found the report, and it's damning. The Communist machine is fully described. I expect MI5 knows a lot about it already, but probably not everything. In particular, one man is identified. I won't tell you his name, but it would be another case of Sir Anthony Blunt."

"And what are you going to do?" Vickie asked quietly.

"I'll spare you all the arguments pro and con, and just give you the outcome. The relevant feature is that this man stopped all his spying years ago. If he's exposed now, it's punishment Old Testament style. Why shouldn't his punishment be his own remorse without public humiliation? I decided this morning that I would tear up the part that refers to him, and I've done just that."

Vickie looked at him in total surprise, and indeed bewilderment. "But the man who wrote the report? He can do it again."

"No," Cranford said sombrely. "There's no chance of that. You probably heard the story some time ago, but couldn't have seen any relevance to all this. Do you remember reading in the papers about a man who died very mysteriously while walking across Waterloo Bridge? All they could find was a mark on his leg which indicated that he'd been stabbed, and they assumed it was with an umbrella point."

"I remember perfectly," Vickie said. "The umbrella point was poisoned, just like in a Sherlock Holmes story."

"The police confirmed this," Cranford said, "but couldn't arrest anybody. The murdered man was known to them as a spy who might be coming in from the cold.

The trouble was that the Communist machine must have decided to act before he revealed things. The story was put out—I've checked this—that the man with the umbrella was from an East European country, I think Bulgaria, who got out of the country instantly, probably just crossing to France on a Channel steamer."

"And what about the man who was mentioned in the report?"

"The police don't have any evidence on him now," Cranford said. "They may have suspected him but there was nothing they could do. I decided to go along with that."

"And this was your moral problem today?" Vickie said. "What decided you?"

Cranford had shrunk back into his chair. "The same feeling that made me decide that my own life has got to be written. I accept the pressure that this puts on me to face the truth, but to expose this man now won't help our cause and would just kill him. It would be a black deed, and I'm not going to do it."

Vickie was silent for a moment. Finally she said: "I don't think I've ever seen someone in the middle of a moral decision like this. I have to say it: I'm very impressed."

"Don't let it affect your general judgment," Cranford said, with something like a twinkle appearing in his eye. "You'll find a lot of awkward things in my life that won't be as clear-cut as this."

"I'm not at all sure if this makes it harder or easier to write the book," Vickie said.

"Oh, I'm not going to lose you now," Cranford said. "I've got your contract all ready, and I want you to sign it before you leave. I regard this book as a fixture. What disturbs me a little is the book I was planning to get done after this one. When I first heard about the report, I thought of commissioning a book at Aston's to deal with the whole treachery story. They think I don't care about books. I was going to show them that I care very much. But now I'm not so sure. I shall probably let the whole project drop, since it might injure the person I've decided to help. If I did the book now, it would probably be just to annoy Miss Marritt."

"The director who has just inherited all those paintings? Where does that fit in?"

Cranford had dropped his sombre mood by now, and was clearly enjoying his decision, and the sharing of it with Vickie. "It's a very funny story," he said. "She's made up her mind to get me to resign as chairman, but I've had a little experience of these things, and I don't think she'll pull it off."

"Why should she want to get rid of you? I assumed you saved the firm by putting in a great deal of money."

"All very true. But now Miss Marritt has all the money she needs to buy me out, and she thinks it will be easy."

"But why should she want to?"

"Oh, of course you don't know," Cranford said. "Her grandfather, Sir William Wren, was the Wren of the title, Aston and Wren. She adored him when she was a little girl. She loved going to his office, which is now my office, so she wants to replace me."

"And you don't intend to let her?"

"There is no way I shall oblige her," Cranford said. "She really missed her chance when young Felix Morgan dealt with that bomb. If he hadn't been around, she might have had an open road, but now the only way to get rid of me would be to have me bumped off American style. Of course she could manage that if she imported a good hit man, but I'm not sure she knows how to set about it. I'll tell you who would help her: my old friend Fred Masolino. I'm sure he knew the going rate for hit men: probably still does. But whether he will help out Miss Marritt is another matter."

In London just a day earlier, as it happened, Miss Rhodine Tonbridge had received a telephone call from her New York friend Tim O'Leary on this very subject. It is fair to say that though she greeted Tim quite warmly, she hadn't the faintest idea what he was conveying in his message.

"Hi, Rhodine!" he had exclaimed. "Got your number from Roop. I'm in London, at the Ritz. Only got a minute. Catching a plane. Got to be back in New York to go jogging in Central Park. Always go jogging on Saturday morning in Central Park."

Rhodine didn't know what he was talking about. Jogging? Was that why he was phoning?"

"Listen, Rhodine," he was saying. "I won't be mentioning any names. Never know who's listening. But you'll understand. Remember what we talked about that night in Harlem? You said your friend could do with a little help. Well I've been asking round. I'm a little out of touch, but it's okay. Will you be in London next week? You will? Good. The person I was thinking of is flying into London next week. Could ring you at your office at noon on Wednesday. Okay for you? Good. I expect you'll fix things up between you. Got to go now. Jog, jog. Okay? Ciao."

He had rung off before Rhodine had a chance to say anything, either in greeting or with a question mark.

6

DETECTIVE SERGEANT THE Hon. Anthony Piers Tesserel-Brougham, second son of the 11th Viscount Calshott, was extremely anxious to present a new theory about Lord Cranford's bomb to his boss, Detective Inspector George Green, but knew in advance that there would be a little hurdle en route. The sergeant recognised that anything linked to his ancestral background had a way of irritating the inspector. In this instance, the link was potent and unavoidable. He would just have to hope that the inspector was not in one of his grumpy moods.

The Honourable Anthony had been visiting his parents over the weekend, staying at their Suffolk place, Tesserel Hall, which was about ten miles from Pelham Court. His father had known Lord Tenderden as a neighbour, but without great affection. Said he was a busybody, with a bee in his bonnet about Communists. Always dropping hints that he was on the track of some top-secret Communist that he was going to expose one day. Maybe he had passed it on to MI5 before he died. More useful now, Anthony thought, if he'd had a line on some top-secret IRA man hovering around with a bomb in his pocket, ready to have another go at Cranford.

No leads seemed to be emerging on this front. Inspector Green had sent Anthony up to Norwich on the Friday to sit in for A.T.—the Anti-Terrorism Branch—at a police and customs discussion on arms smuggling through East Anglian ports. Interesting as background, but no more. Green had readily agreed that he should stay on, as his parents lived nearby, to have a look round informally. "Double things up," he had said with slight sarcasm, as if to indicate that for his part he was going to count on the routine Cranford surveillance. Anthony saw it differently. Simenon often presented Maigret as putting routine on one side to delve into personal relationships, with startling results. He would do the same here, by exploiting local friendships. A good way to start was by dropping in at the Pelham Arms for a drink before lunch on Saturday, keeping his ears open for anything the regulars might be saying about the bomb that had nearly wiped out the lord of the manor.

He had done just this and it had worked. A theory had emerged which grew straight out of his personal standing at the pub, where they knew him well. Not only was he almost a local there, he was a local with an Hon. attached. More important still, he played cricket for the village team whenever work permitted.

It was some time since he had been there, and the regulars made a fuss of him. "Works at Scotland Yard" he heard someone say in pride. If the inspector had sent a constable from A.T. who was also in the area, he didn't seem to be around at the Pelham Arms.

There was some talk in the pub of the bomb sent to Cranford, with plenty of conventional disgust with the IRA but with no one aware, it seemed, that Anthony's field at Scotland Yard gave him a special interest. A more general topic was the festival, due to open in ten days' time; what mattered most on this was the festival cricket match with nearby Lazenby on the Saturday afternoon. Bill Chatterton, captain of the Ashenham team, soon spotted him and came over quickly to secure a promise to play. Anthony said he wasn't sure if he would be free, but would try. "Nice to be back," he added. "Nothing changes, I see. George Sekelis still running everything."

A great shout of laughter had come from the large

table across the room at which tankards were being raised in gratitude, it seemed, to the genial Sekelis sitting there. "Life and soul of the party," Chatterton agreed. "You *will* try to come? Lazenby have got a new first-class batsman who works at the local garage. We need you. After all, you did play for Oxford."

"I'm very rusty now," Anthony said. "Of course, if I'm free I'd love to play."

Looking up, he saw George Sekelis on his way over, tankard in hand. "Anthony, my boy. Where have you been? I hope Bill has roped you in for the festival match. Crime must take a rest that weekend."

It was impossible to resist the joviality. Part of it was the strange accent, presumably Bulgarian. Sekelis rolled the r's, as in "crime" and "rest," to quite fearful effect.

"You're down here on the bomb business, I suppose?" Sekelis always knew everything by instinct, Anthony thought. But of course. How else had he built up such a successful antiques business?

"I'm investigating the festival," he replied cheerfully. "What goes on this year?"

"You mean apart from the cricket match? Well, there's one absolutely marvellous thing, really great." "Great" came out with a superb flourish of the r. "Imagine—the Guarneri Quartette are playing Opus 135 on the Friday evening. You must plan to come. And you've heard about the play this year: an adaptation of *Les Liaisons Danger-euses,* or some scenes from it. Lord Cranford's wife Margaretta is in it, with a very good Irish actor called Patrick Hearn. It should be interesting for all kinds of reasons, from what I hear. Listen—are you free after lunch for an hour or so? One of the lads told me—he works on the lighting—that they've got a rehearsal this afternoon in one of the stables that's fitted out for this. I'm going to go along and listen. Why don't you come with me?"

With George Sekelis, one didn't ask about permissions and all that. At three o'clock they were sitting on some makeshift chairs in the stable, watching the actors rehearsing with scripts in their hands. Anthony hadn't read the original book; George had, of course, and gave him a quick resumé. Two aristocrats, a Marquise and a Viscount, former lovers, get their fun now in manipulating other people with total immorality. "They're setting it in Ireland instead of eighteenth-century France," he said, "which is why they've adopted this Irish accent. Very good idea: the Anglo-Irish aristocracy was as decadent as the French. And don't the two of them look splendid? One begins to believe the rumours."

Margaretta and Patrick: Countess and Viscount in the adaptation. One could easily guess what the gossip had been saying about this handsome pair, but beyond the obvious talk of something going on, Anthony began to feel a deeper issue. As characters in the play they were at the same time cynical and exultant, totally amoral but sincere in the posture they had adopted. After a few minutes of the dialogue, one began to believe that the play echoed an outlook—a relationship—that might be true for them in real life. For people of spirit like them, life had no meaning unless one set oneself an impossible task and pulled it off. To enjoy life, one had to get away with murder. Was this what had appealed to Cranford's wife in choosing the play?

"I must read the book," he said to Sekelis. "Is it as persuasive as this?"

"Much more," Sekelis said. "Immensely elegant, and funny, but it's also very serious. It's a great love story in which they have to outdo each other in being outrageous, using other people as props or dummies to secure points for deception just for the thrill. The contrast is beautiful. Outwardly, they are respectable members of society. Inwardly, they are very different: a double life.

But, you know, I've always thought that a double life must be very rewarding if one carries it to the extreme."

"And how does it end?"

Sekelis was smiling as if enjoying a joke in his own way. "There's a pretend-ending in which their wickedness is punished, of course I don't believe things end this way. There's no end, in fact. While the conjuror keeps the balls in the air, it is a lovely game. No one cares what happens after."

Anthony left after a while to go home. Some cousins were coming to tea, and he'd promised his mother to show up. It was as he was driving that the theory took shape which he was now anxious to present to Inspector Green.

In all the police work so far, the letter-bomb had been treated as a straightforward part of the IRA campaign. The material and the form of construction had been certified by Commander Winterton as similar enough to make this the best working hypothesis, despite some differences that he held to be minor in significance. The claim for responsibility had come from what seemed like a splinter IRA organization, but that too was reconcilable. The detailed police work had followed these lines, but had produced nothing useful. As no one had been actually harmed, there was no large cash reward publicized to stimulate those ready to grass.

Two things had now triggered Anthony's mind into a wholly different approach—two things plus a course in criminal psychology at the Open University. The course was going to be a particular stumbling block in getting the inspector to look at his theory at all favourably. When Anthony had seen the course described in the Open University Handbook and promptly registered, he had felt it unwise to mention it to his superior of the time, who was as blinkered as Green himself was sure to be on such matters. You'll get nothing out of psychology books, was the view they took. Those so-called experts sitting at universities and writing books haven't any experience to draw on. Experience is the only way to learn. Stuffing your head full of theories will just stifle the practical training you'll be getting at the Inspector's Training Course.

But he had persisted, not as an extra qualification for promotion but because he found it enjoyable as a *relief* from experience. The most interesting part was in lessons drawn from cultural anthropology, and within this, the detailed study that had concentrated on the attitude to crime of the Partridge Islanders of the South Pacific. One could imagine the inspector's dislike for this simply on principle, how much more distasteful as an element in explaining a case he was actually engaged in.

The tiny island of the South Pacific bearing the name of Sir Ralph Partridge had been discovered by him in 1772, two years after Captain Cook discovered (or took over) Australia, but the traders and missionaries had passed it by without involvement, so that when American anthropologists finally heard about it and moved in around 1925, they found primitivism untouched. Their key discovery in relation to what went on in this Garden of Eden was not in the realm of sex, as in the somewhat discredited theories of Margaret Mead, but murder. According to the Open University lecturer, an understanding of the Partridge Islanders might force us to come to terms with concealed motivations in our own culture. The issue was that murder for the Islanders had no relation to passion or violence. Murder was a way of dying for the benefit, one might say, of the social system. If a young man and woman wanted to pursue their lives together, they celebrated this, or gave themselves social permission, by "helping" a parent to die. There was some argument among the academics about the details, but all agreed that it took one back at a bound to a motive for murder that must lie deep in human nature, since it was authenticated from a time when nature' had not yet been overlaid by the taboos that society had developed against most forms of killing. Anthony had found this very liberating to read about in a book and authenticated in a vivid way when he was introduced to the attitudes embodied in *Les Liaisons Dangereuses.* The countess and viscount in the play had already shaken off all the old taboos. The whole point of their life together was to execute an act that we would now think outrageous, and get away with it. A bomb at the festival, Anthony decided, must now lie ahead.

It was called for in anthropological theory and could be spelt out in specific detail. A great hint was that the actor playing the viscount was Irish. An ardent Catholic Irishman looking for outrage would find a blow against the English the most satisfying form, and if this was to be expressed by a bomb, what better timing that during the festival? In living out the play, Lady Cranford, his partner in outrage, would go along with anything proposed, simply to express their joint disdain for conventional morality. In the deepest sense, what they planned was not antisocial. On the contrary, it spoke for the most natural instincts of society, long buried but true to nature nonetheless; they were demonstrating this by putting on a play that reached back into human nature in an open and convincing way. Even without practical gain, an "incident" like a bomb would be enjoyable for its own sake, something the Open University lecturer had called an *acte gratuit,* far the most subtle form of pleasure. But there might be more if, in this case, there was a bomb that had the effect of removing Lord Cranford. This would be quite acceptable to the daredevil couple as an *acte gratuit* that also happened to be worth at least a million pounds to the surviving widow. No Partridge

111

Islander would want more than this as a way to a happy ending.

Oh, the joys of theorising! Anthony felt as if he were back at Oxford, reading for the first time a popular summary of the dream theories of Sigmund Freud. Surely the inspector would see the beauty of the argument. There might be a few loose ends, but wasn't it on the right track, and in Maigret style? At ten on Monday morning he was ready to expound, and strange to say, the inspector seemed quite impressed.

"Very interesting," the inspector said. "The argument for a bomb at the festival is very convincing. Constable Fulton came in to see me about this when you were away at the Norwich discussion. I gave him a break from the London surveillance of Cranford to have a look round the area you've just been in, Pelham Court, and he's had quite a few ideas. Told me about the play, and the Irishman Patrick Hearn in the lead. Very suggestive. We'll have to work out a few plans for festival time. I got on to Belfast on Friday to see if they could tell me anything useful about Hearn. Not very helpful, I'm afraid. Apparently he's a typical Protestant from an old Protestant family living near Cork. A lot of the old English live down there, you know. It looks as if this particular Irishman doesn't care much for the IRA. I was also wondering how your theory calling for a new bomb relates to the first one that came through the post. Not much connection as far as I could see. Still, it's something worth thinking about."

He was being rather fruity in tone for some reason, but in a good mood, feet on awful desk. "That course you've been taking—what did you call it? Cultural anthropology, I think you said. Sounds very interesting. My wife took a course a couple of years ago at the Tottenham Polytechnic on electrical mechanics for the home. Amazingly useful. She can repair anything. Saves a fortune. I wish I had done it myself."

He took his feet off the desk for a moment to reach into a drawer and pull out some notes that he seemed to have got ready for his sergeant, but first he went on talking for a moment in a reflective style. "Cultural anthropology," he murmured. "Murder in the Stone Age. Good title for a detective story: 'A Stone Age Murder.' I had just one thought about it. If that was the pattern of life in the Stone Age, obviously every Stone Age policeman would have to study it, but as we're not in the Stone Age now, shouldn't we policemen study our own cultural patterns? For example, what about the weekly murder rota in the *News of the World?* I read it carefully every Sunday. I'm sure you do, too. No?" He had seen Anthony shake his head. "Well, try it. It's our own cultural anthropology. Yes, you'd get a lot out of the *News of the World* reports.

"Mind you," he went on, "I'm not saying that your theory is all wrong. Tell you an odd thing. It seems *half* right, but that can be just as confusing, like putting the left glove on the right hand. The play, and the Irishman and all that. There's something right about it, but I don't know what it is."

Anthony glowed a little. This was the inspector in an agreeable mood. Just have to get the glove on the correct hand and proceed from there. Or was he leading up to a crusher?

"Have to watch it a little," he was saying. "Abstract theory can leave you high and dry. A ton of theory against an ounce of fact. Got a few new facts to play with, as it happens. Came in on Friday." For the first time he smiled broadly. Here it comes, Anthony thought.

"There's something quite new in the picture," the inspector was saying. "New to us, that is. Came in from Grovel, just when we needed it."

"Grovel" was the Scotland Yard nickname for information, usually scandalous, that was phoned in to them regularly by a host of insiders who sent material in, for financial gain, to the scandal-sheet *Private Eye*, but who often passed the word round also, for reasons of self-importance, to Scotland Yard people they could trust. "Grovel" was the name of a column in *Private Eye* full of assorted gossip, but among the innuendos there was usually a grain of fact, often useful to Scotland Yard when checked out, especially if it fitted in with things they already knew or suspected. The procedure meant that they would usually get their snippet of scandal before it appeared in *Private Eye*, which would put them on the alert for quick anticipation or followups. This had happened in the present case, and the inspector was clearly delighted. It had amused him to give his cock-a-doodle sergeant a free run with his crazy anthropological theories, but now they could get down to business.

"The Grovel bit would be just funny," he said to Anthony, "except that we've got something more serious about it from another source. Grovel's hint is about a woman director of Cranford's publishing company who would be very happy if someone bumped him off. The gossip around the company, Aston and Wren, is that this woman, Miss Emilia Marritt, wants to become chairman very badly because she's a granddaughter of one of the founders, Sir William Wren. She hadn't the slightest chance, but suddenly she's come into a fortune. She's the woman who inherited a collection of paintings in America. You must have read about it in the papers."

"Yes, I did. You mean she can now offer to buy out Cranford?"

"He'd never sell, so she'd like to see him have a serious accident, say with the help of a hit man."

Anthony burst out laughing. "Did Grovel say this?"

"No, just told us of the rumours in the company about

114

manoeuvres for the top job. If there was no hit man around, it would just be background. But as it happens, I have now had a message from our old friend in the FBI that a hit man is on his way here for this precise purpose."

Anthony almost leapt out of his chair. "You mean, Zeb! Zeb has been in touch? On this?"

Inspector Green was now beaming with satisfaction. "Zeb and no other. I had a phone call from him at 2 A.M. on Saturday morning. He had rung the Yard and they gave him my home number. All he said was: 'Can you get to the office? Can't talk on an open line.' It took me an hour. I was cursing him all the time, but when I got through to him on the Red Line, I had to agree it was worth all the trouble. They had had a message from an FBI agent they keep in Amsterdam. A well-known New York gangster that the FBI keep track of had showed up in Amsterdam two days earlier and was now on the way to London. Zeb wanted me to know immediately in case we could move in. This man is what you might call a free-lance, works on contracts."

"So there *are* hit men," Anthony muttered, a little self-consciously. "I never knew how much to believe."

"Oh, you can believe it," Green said. "You wouldn't suspect Zeb of pulling my leg, would you, just to get me out of bed at two in the morning?"

Anthony was trying to hold on to his wits. "But with a contract from this woman?" he said disbelievingly. "You surely don't mean that Zeb knows of an actual contract."

"Not a hundred percent, he says, but near enough to worry about. They have agents everywhere picking up stories, and they've been putting them together. It's firm in one sense. Zeb says when Miss Marritt was in New York recently to see about her paintings, there was talk with this gangster on this precise subject. One of Zeb's men picked up the story, and it's now being taken to stage two."

Anthony shook his head in disbelief. "It still sounds very vague. Is there no more proof?"

"The proof comes out in what Zeb told me on the phone. Miss Marritt hasn't worked on the plan herself; it's being handled by her close friend—and I mean very close friend—who went with her to New York. Her name is Miss Rhodine Tonbridge. She works in advertising, in London, and has contacts with some of our villains here. It looks as if she asked one of them for a contact in New York who might know how to organise things. She was given a name, and talked to this man in New York. You can guess who it was."

"The man who showed up in Amsterdam, on the way to London."

"Exactly. He's called Tim O'Leary."

"Did he come and get in touch with Miss Rhodine?"

"A very fleeting visit. The FBI were looking for him, lost track for a few days, and then found him at the Ritz on Friday, ready to leave for New York. All the American gangsters stay at the Ritz—they like the Casino—so the FBI keep a man watching the phone there. Quite illegal, but we don't say anything. Well, on Friday he rang Miss Rhodine, not from his room, but from a callbox downstairs. The FBI man picked up most of it through that radio they use. What did emerge was that 'a friend' would be getting in touch with her about meeting on Wednesday."

"Not very firm," Anthony ventured. "Could be just a tourist friend."

"Could be," the inspector agreed, "but we'll keep an eye on who she sees on Wednesday. Something usually happens after O'Leary's been around."

"Did anything happen in Amsterdam?"

"Yes, something did happen in Amsterdam. There was a body in one of the canals."

"But why don't they pick up O'Leary?"

"Because they can never pin anything on him. Things happen after he's left a place. Zeb thinks he sets things up, like an agent, and keeps his distance. Probably got a lot of men working for him in various spots: just picks on someone who doesn't leave a track."

"But this time we have a link, through this man who's meeting Miss Rhodine on Wednesday?"

"And you can bet your last button that we're not going to let him slip through our fingers. Time we did the FBI a good turn. What's up? You look a bit disappointed. Cultural anthropology out of the window, eh? Back to ordinary police work? Well, if you don't like it, I do. Nice little joint operation with the Americans. Suits me down to the ground."

Anthony was still struggling with his bewilderment. Somehow or other he could accept a wild theory based on an analogy with the Partridge Islanders, but not that a man with a gun could point it at Lord Cranford and blow a hole in his head, as Elmore Leonard would put it. It was Elmore Leonard versus Simenon. In Simenon, the *idée maîtresse* is ultimately cultural, so one believes it. In Elmore Leonard's books, there's nothing to believe in: it's just a question of ballistics. Bang, and Lord Cranford is dead. Very crude compared with Simenon. It offends everything, not to mention the horror of a killing in one of London's most famous publishing houses.

"The woman must be a monster," he found himself saying. "What can justify it? She's a director of a famous company, and she's come into a fortune. Why should she get involved with murder?"

The inspector eased his sitting position—feet on desk—in total satisfaction. "I thought you'd explained this yourself," he said to Anthony, with only the faintest hint of irony. "Isn't it cultural anthropology? Ordinary killings are for money, or revenge, or just explosions of anger. But here we've got the strongest of motives: the urge to be chief of the tribe. Doesn't this show up in the Open University course? Plenty of evidence, surely, even without your funny old Islanders. When we used to read the Bible in Sunday class at our chapel, it was full of stories about one person after another killing everyone within range to become chief of the tribe. The deepest natural instinct, you would say, wouldn't you?"

Anthony looked at him ruefully. This was not his day. First, Constable Fulton, operating around the Pelham Court village without benefit of a social position, had brought back all the relevant information about the festival and the actors. And now the ordinary police machine had produced the story of a hit-man operation against Lord Cranford that might settle everything without a bomb at the festival. No—it wasn't his day.

He looked at the stolid figure now unwinding his feet from the top of the desk and asked himself if this wasn't one more mystery that he had to cope with. Could anyone look as dull as the inspector and yet be so effective? His mind went back to something the inspector had said when the subject of cultural anthropology had been forced on him, something about getting an answer wrong by putting the right glove on the left hand. It had just emerged spontaneously, but it seemed to have a significant meaning that lingered with one. How to apply it? He wished he knew.

Vickie was making her preparations. The time had come for the first visit to Yorkshire, and she hardly knew why she was so excited about it. It was a sheer coincidence that nothing had taken her there before this, though it had a legendary quality in conversation. From what she had heard, one entered a different world, some said, as the train moved out of King's Cross Station; and, all agreed, after passing Watford. The symbol of it for her was not Yorkshire Pudding but the ruddy scrubbed look in the faces of Yorkshiremen she had met.

Mixed up with this was the excitement she felt burgeoning within her as a new historical subject began to open up. The economic history studies she had delved into already gave her a framework for the huge swings in industry that had dominated the period in which Cranford's business had expanded, and she had already immersed herself in a number of books from the London Library on the experience of some of the major companies. What she lacked was any appreciation of what one might call the psychological landscape. In reading history at Oxford she had taken the industrial expansion of Midwest America as a special subject, and had quickly acquired a feeling for its shape: a single drive gathering momentum without letup; one could write about it quite fairly in personal, almost romantic, terms. This had been equally true, in a different way, when she came to evaluate the opening up of virginal South Africa in the days of the great Kruger. In both cases, there had been a constant flow of new people coming in from outside. Would the Yorkshire of the young Herbert Thomson emerge with the same clarity? Somehow she anticipated a more bitty, almost higgledy-piggledy background here, a maze of old and new workshops, a scattering of worn-out factories offset by occasional masses of chimneys, with the local population deeply entrenched and reflecting the grime and weariness of past generations, with little obvious excitement for what was new. Some of this had come through in her conversations with Cranford, yet little that brought colour into his own origins. Obviously he must have held some key to open a door to expansion, but he had not identified it, preferring to talk much more of his later triumphs, the rearmament phase of the later 1930s, the wartime boom, and then the astonishing development of industrial amalgamations after the war in which he must have expressed something like genius.

The archives lodged in the Chesham Square hideout had not yielded much more so far on the very early period, though she had some names to go on, recorded already in her notebooks. It had been quite a disappointment to find that Felix Morgan was also rather uninformed on the early days. She had had a grand dinner with him on the night before she left, in which he had been vastly entertaining with his talk of the role of a troubleshooter both in U.S. business and in Europe. Though he had begun to work for Cranford less than a year before, she had rather assumed that things would have emerged in conversations that he might now pass on. If anything, the position seemed to be just the reverse. He had quizzed her quite a bit on the archives and what they showed, giving her a feeling that he would himself have liked to browse in them if he'd had the chance. She had been very restrained on this, of course, in the light of the assurance of confidentiality that Cranford had laid down.

It had not inhibited their conversation, for Felix—as she was now calling him—had a fund of anecdotes himself, on his early life in Chicago, where he had grown up, and on the vagaries of work for huge American concerns. He was amazed to find her so well informed, from her Oxford paper, on the character of industrial expansion in the Midwest.

"You know so much about the world," he had said, "and yet I suppose it was all on paper. Didn't you ever want to go out and see it with your own eyes?"

"Not at that stage," she said. "It's ridiculous, really, I quite agree, to build up a picture in one's head this way. I got an Alpha Plus for the paper, and that was enough. Of course it was very different when I did the Kruger book. There I had to go and live in the landscape; even the very old things came to life in a real way."

"And now you're going to do this for Yorkshire?" he said. "I'm dying to hear what you'll find. Will you tell me? We could have dinner when you get back. Will you?"

How lively and spontaneous he was. An age ago, it now seemed, she had wondered whether there was room in him for Ambrose's theory of double identity. She had to smile now. It wasn't just his good looks and bright blond hair. Looks didn't matter, as she had found out during her long attachment to Laurence. No one could have called Laurence good-looking. He was rather plump, his eyes were narrow, and his hair, brown and wispy, had already begun to fall back toward baldness. But she had loved being with him.

It was in sitting opposite Felix that she had found herself taking Laurence apart, though without positive rancour, just irritated that she had given him so much and been let down. She felt aware, too, how life had suddenly opened up for her when Felix had come on the scene. That first news item on the BBC had proved to be a true bombshell in her life. She had been locked up in Laurence because of the intense experience of the attachment but without exchanging experience in any full sense. Ruefully, she knew that this was the fate of all women who had affairs with married men. Watch it, she felt like warning them all, knowing that they would never listen, as she had not. She had felt sometimes that she had caught a warning in Ambrose Usher's eyes when they had been together. Dear Ambrose: he knew everything, without imposing himself. What will he see in Felix? she wondered. Something different from what she saw, perhaps.

The talk with Felix about America had somehow brought Ambrose into her consciousness. He knew America so well that he would probably see Felix in his true context, a setting that was beyond her, despite her paper on the Midwest. By all accounts, Ambrose had America in his bloodstream, reacting like the new machines he had talked about—psychological computers—that could unfold the buried background of every American. What a pity she couldn't apply this to unravelling young Herbert Thomson's early life in deepest Yorkshire. We have the Parish Registers in England and in abundance; perhaps they were being computerized, too, but this was still thin static material compared with the lively background that would be fed into the American computers—the unceasing movements in the population, the constant inflows and outflows, and the changing patterns in agriculture, industry, and commerce—all grist to the computer's mill. The thought brought her back to Shilton, the base she had chosen in which to launch her safari. She had to smell the Yorkshire air for herself, even if the raw material might be scrappy. Perhaps that was the real lesson to be learnt: to slow down to the northern pace so as to enjoy the traditional attitudes—and dishes—they were all said to be attached to.

If she managed to get talking to some of the old survivors, it would have to be under a general cover, say a projected series for the BBC on the depression. She had decided to start at Shilton, the first place mentioned in Cranford's *Who's Who* entry as the jumping-off point for his future triumphs. He had been lively enough, when they talked, about how he had first started with the Baxby company, enlarged in time to Baxby and Thomson. It was this setting that she wanted to explore, to get the feel of a small South Yorkshire town in that far-off time, ready to fit it in with what Cranford might tell her later. She would play it by ear, to see what emerged.

* * *

The historian accepts that however hard one works on
the factual background, the reward comes from something unexpected. Emanuel Baxby was the proof. She
had concentrated on facts for a full day after her arrival
at Shilton's grim little railway station, still standing at the
bottom end of the town. For a few hours she had turned
the pages of old newspapers and directories extracted
for her from the cellar of the dingy public library, opened
in 1910, as the plaque outside proudly proclaimed, by
the Earl of Sandbach. The musty look of the papers was
only part of the story, more dominantly one was aware
of a dying heritage both in the library and the narrow
streets outside. There was a smell of bleakness in the
main street with its mixture of small locally owned shops
interlaced with co-ops and a few branches of national
names like Lipton's. The money pattern swung dully
between building societies and betting-shops. The mood
seemed frugal even at the pubs, where the regulars
seemed content to sit silently for a long time with one
glass in front of them. Modernity—TV and video—glit-
tered here and there in a town that had otherwise become
an ill-preserved museum.

But even at this stage she was learning. She had
persuaded a taxi driver at the station to drive her round
for an hour to a few factory sites, old and new, and then
through a variety of narrow, terraced streets of small
brick houses in which young Herbert Thomson had
doubtless lived as an infant, clattering off to school,
maybe in clogs, and then rising to something like financial independence in the jobs that followed his first task
of sweeping the factory floors for five shillings a week.
She had quickly picked up a few of the local industrial
names, and could see the process of change in large
areas of empty land, sometimes just derelict, and at other
times cluttered with some small car parks.

Once she had got her bearings, she would try to assess where Baxby and Thomson had fitted in. It was already clear how joining Baxby's had been the significant step up the ladder for young Herbert. Even a quick tour soon produced the evidence. Turning a corner in an area now looking far from prosperous, she had spotted a row of houses called "Baxby Street." "Is there still a Baxby family?" she had asked her taxi driver. Indeed there was, he told her, with a small factory close by. He had accepted her in the role of a journalist writing on the area, and promptly took her to the factory, a neat little building with the Baxby name over the door. To set up a meeting she had stopped at a telephone booth nearby and extracted the telephone number from Information. Mr. Baxby's secretary had answered. She would ask Mr. Baxby if he was free to see Miss McKenzie the next day for a talk on the history of the area. And there, on the next day, she was.

She was not to know until much later how crucial the encounter was to the story that was unfolding, but even in itself it was a moment that suddenly concentrated everything the way a large old-fashioned bag used to be pulled together by strings. Outside, Shilton was a dreary echo of the past; here, when she sat down in Mr. Baxby's room and heard his story, she got a picture of industry very much alive in a small, intimate way, with products designed to fit a myriad specialized purposes, calling on a vast variety of the special steels for which the area was famous, and engineered with consummate skill to fit the ancillary needs of large-scale industry. Photographs showed how elaborate and bizarre these products could be, but if they had no glamour in themselves, they still had a good safe place in the scheme of things. And if a modest factory was to survive at this level, it was in the person of a man like Emanuel Baxby, its current head.

A cup of coffee had been brought in, with digestive

biscuits on the side. Baxby looked around thirty-five, well dressed in a dark business suit, with no trace of a northern accent and nothing in his face to suggest the scrubbed Yorkshire look of the man, presumably an ancestor, whose picture—a large photograph—was mounted on the wall. As a further sign of change, it soon emerged that the current Baxby had been at Cambridge University where he got a degree in economics, and had himself been contemplating writing a study of the industrial history of the region, with special reference to the Depression. His interest in what she was herself working on was so strong that she felt very deceptive in having to leave out her particular concern with the experience, years ago, of the young Herbert Thomson. But this came up anyhow from the side, in discussing the history of Baxby's; here what he had to say was to prove central to her research, once she had taken in what it indicated.

The picture on the wall was, indeed, of his grandfather, born in 1865. Grandfather's father had opened a workshop in 1870 for repairing spindles in an ingenious mechanical process that got over the need to take them all apart, and this grew, in Grandfather's hands, into a substantial factory, serving a wide area in working special steels, using patented processes largely imported from Germany. "They were way ahead already," Baxby said. "By the turn of the century there were many crucial processes in metalworking that English companies had to experiment in if they wanted to maintain their position. My father went on with this and learnt his lesson the hard way, or, shall I say, got the best and worst of it. He had worked as an apprentice to a metal company in Düsseldorf, and adapted many of their practices when he came back and ultimately took over the company. The firm grew. My father was mayor of Shilton, and they wanted him to go into Parliament. But then something unpredictable happened. A young man called Herbert

Thomson joined the company. Father was very excited to have him because he brought with him some quite revolutionary patents he had invented and developed in a small workshop for shaping the most intricate cutting tools in very hard steels like vanadium or manganese alloys, turning lengthy hand processes into continuous operations that could be applied to very large-scale companies. After settling down and pushing the new methods still further under Father's guidance, they made young Thomson a partner, and then they really got going. It's safe to say that all metal companies today use some adaptations of the changes we introduced on the basis of Thomson's patents. The man was undoubtedly a natural engineering genius to have thought this up and got it going in what must have been a tiny workshop before he came to us, so it was a real combination worthy of a partnership: he had had the genius idea, and we had the factory and background to take it forward. But then something terrible happened: everything fell apart."

Vickie felt a tingling within her to have struck oil so wonderfully and so naturally. Keeping her voice as calm as she could, she put in a tentative question as Baxby broke off to take a sip of his coffee.

"Was it the Depression that broke things up?" she asked.

"Well, yes and no," Baxby said. "Of course the Depression was a disaster for the area as a whole, but our company would have been all right. In fact you could say that it *was* all right: it just wasn't *our* company anymore. I'm sure you know that our partner Thomson was on his way to becoming the great Lord Cranford, and we were just one of the steppingstones. No Depression for Herbert Thomson," he said sardonically. "He just went up and up on his own. As far as I know, Lord Cranford is pretty well the biggest international operator in the world today. If you were interested . . ."

"Oh, I'm very interested," Vickie said. "It's fascinating."

"Well, I can tell you more, though I have to watch my step. Lord Cranford is still alive, though he must be nearly eighty, I suppose, so if I say something critical and it gets back to him, he might think it libellous. I'm sure he thought that everything that happened was very proper. It just felt rather different from the Baxby end. You do get many changes in business operations, changes of ownership and influence and all that. If someone does very well out of it, the other person is inclined to feel sore, as you can imagine. However, I'll be very careful. Perhaps I'll just tell you the outline and let you draw your own conclusions, rightly or wrongly. After all, you had to do this sort of thing in that marvellous book of yours on Kruger."

"You know my book?" Vickie began to glow a little as she always did when the book came in for praise without warning.

"Lovely book," Baxby said. "It suddenly occurred to me when we were talking that you must be *the* Victoria McKenzie."

"I'm very pleased," Vickie murmured. "Thank you."

"So I can leave you to add things up yourself if I tell you what happened without dotting the i's and crossing the t's. The business had inevitably started going down at the bad point in the Depression. As my father told the story, Thomson came forward one day with the proposal that they should sell out to a much larger firm to cut losses. He said he'd been looking round and had found a very good option, offering either a large cash sum or a small scale grant of stock. He recommended the cash option and my father agreed. But then Thomson changed his mind and took shares in the other company, and this was just before the big rearmament boom began. Shall I spell things out further?"

"I don't think you need to."

"Just a little thing I'd mention, with what you might call social implications. My father took cash because he wanted me and my two brothers to go to a very expensive school—Harrow, in fact—and then on to Oxford or Cambridge. He wouldn't have been able to finance this and his other social plans otherwise. For our education, he put a large sum into endowment policies for the three of us. He wanted us to have the advantages that he'd missed. He also bought a very large house, with stables and horses, so we could advance socially. Oh, he achieved that all right. My brothers and I took off on an upwardly mobile *social* curve, absolutely the opposite of the really meaningful upward *industrial* curve that he had expressed by being apprenticed to an advanced metal firm in Germany. It's ironic, isn't it? I was being taught to belong to the top social class without any resources to give it validity. If my father had seen through Thomson's advice, he could have held on through the post-war boom and then sent us on to these high-falutin' schools in real style . . ."

"As Thomson probably did," Vickie ventured.

"That's *your* assessment," Baxby said with a twinkle. "I would never make such an allegation, of course."

"What about the company that bought you out? Did Thomson have any interest . . ."

Baxby looked at her and paused for a moment. "I'd better not say anything on that," he muttered. "It's all over now anyhow."

"But you have restarted your business?"

"Father did when weapons became A-1 priority during the war. He built a little factory here to serve war industries, but then he fell ill and died. It had to close, but after the war and Cambridge, I decided to try and make a go of it myself, *in piam memoriam.*"

"And it worked?"

128

"I've kept the name alive. There's a Baxby Street in the town, and there's a Baxby factory to go with it."

"And your brothers?"

"Oh, they didn't have the same sentiment. One went off to Canada after the war and the other to Australia. Good old British Empire."

"And how do you assess Thomson now that it's all over?"

"I don't. I try to be philosophic in a neutral way. Business is full of this sort of thing. If Cranford just used us rather skillfully and emerged with everything we'd owned, it's probably not the only occasion. If I may quote Andrew Marvell: 'The same arts that did gain/A power, must it maintain.' " Of course he was a Cambridge poet—you don't have to accept him at Oxford."

Inside the office it was like a Common Room, with coffee and digestive biscuits circulating instead of port. Outside the room, as he led her to the front door, she heard the subdued clatter and clangs of a small factory, and caught a glimpse of overhead traction, moving carriers, and individual parts across the open space; an agreeable kind of factory, small enough for the participants to remain human. She envisaged a wholly different atmosphere in Thomson's subsequent empire, with companies bought and sold by distant speculators, unwilling—and indeed unable—to consider human participants in the huge enterprises that changed hands in the City for pieces of paper. That was a skill, too, as Cranford had shown. In his case, the personal element had finally surfaced in his decision to have the story of his business life given coherent form, regardless of whether it showed grievous immoralities en route. She had to agree with Baxby that if Thomson had behaved fiercely—even cruelly—in looking after his own interests in this case, it was likely to reflect a set pattern in his business style: *the same arts* and all that.

129

A taxi had been summoned to take her to the public library, where she planned to delve again into the old directories, but en route she passed a school and had a sudden impulse to see if she could glimpse here how the child had been father to the man. It was an ancient building, the only old "elementary" school of the town, according to the taxi driver.

The headmaster received her very civilly when she said that she was writing about the period of the Depression and had had an interesting talk with Mr. Baxby.

"A very fine family," the headmaster said. "It's very good that he restarted the family business to give the chance of a job to boys from the school. They've always done that, of course. His father was the mayor, and there's a Baxby Street in the town, which is very nice, don't you think? Preserves a sense of tradition and service. I always tell the boys this. It gives them something to look up to."

"Some of your pupils must have risen to very important positions over the years," Vickie suggested.

"Yes, indeed. A very distinguished tradition in every field."

"I suppose Lord Cranford is one of your prime examples. He's risen so high."

"Cranford? The big industrialist? He wasn't at the school."

"He was Herbert Thomson before he got the title, a partner of Mr. Baxby's father in Baxby and Thomson."

"Oh, was he? Well, Thomson is a very common name. But he was not at the school, or we would have put his name on the board when he got so famous."

"It's the only old elementary school in the area, isn't it?" Vickie asked. "Would that have been true when Thomson was a boy, say in the 1920s?"

The headmaster seemed to take her query as an insult. "I think I can say that I know all the old pupils who've become famous," he said, with his Yorkshire accent getting a bit rougher. "The Baxby partner was never here."

Vickie was beginning to get intrigued at this strange and unlooked-for development. "Perhaps he came from a school nearby," she said. "Like a village school."

She couldn't think at first why she was persisting, but something in the story seemed wrong. As for the headmaster, he had clearly had enough.

"I think we know our own area best," he said sharply. "If this partner had come from our area we would have got his help for scholarships. Whoever it was who joined Baxby's company must have come from somewhere else."

He was obviously right, and Vickie caved in politely. She had realised, as he was speaking, that she'd fallen into a simple trap—and perhaps an intended one—when she assumed that Cranford had come from Shilton in the first instance. The source she had drawn on, *Who's Who*, had simply said, as she now recalled: "Born in Yorkshire 1910. Partner, Baxby and Thomson, 1935–7," before going on with an endless list of other company involvements. But why just "Yorkshire" and not his place of birth? She would ask him when the time came to discuss the facts and the impressions she was accumulating. She had assumed that by identifying his origin as "Yorkshire" he was just pointing to a central fact in his life. But perhaps he had a reason for not being more specific.

In the train, settling down at six for the journey to London, with a glass of wine accompanying her meal very agreeably, she looked at the passing landscape with feelings wholly different from those of the journey only two days earlier. A new world had come to life in these two days, and very satisfying it was. Even the chimneys were now generating a sense of well-being as they gave off smoke and some flashing fire here and there in the early evening air. She saw the train now as an artery of this ancient world. If the houses and factories lay along the line with no set pattern, the people who lived among them had signalled a very satisfying variety. A special prize in this field had to go to the headmaster, who claimed to know the name of every boy in his school over the last sixty years and challenged her to dispute it. More seriously, she knew where she was now, having found a way into this hitherto distant land, with impressions she would be able to draw on in the early part of the book. Not that it hadn't raised a rather peculiar question about the very early days of her subject that she would want to look into.

Oddly enough, it was a question that Ambrose seemed to find particularly intriguing when she had a word with him that night. He had telephoned her quite late, with many apologies, to see how she had got on in Yorkshire. He was very interested in the Baxby story, and laughed aloud when she told him about the headmaster.

"You never picked up anything from Felix Morgan about Cranford's childhood?" he asked her.

"No, not a word. In fact Felix is very curious about it himself. Asked me quite a lot of questions, really probing ones."

"Did he now?" Ambrose said. "That's very interesting, isn't it?"

It was nice talking to Ambrose, however late the hour. He always seemed to be suggesting things you might guess yourself if you were as bright as he was. This, as it happened, was one of those occasions. When Ambrose had expounded his ideas about double identity, Vickie had fought shy of applying it personally, as—say—to her new friend Morgan. Ambrose, alert to anything odd that seemed to surface, had no such inhibitions. Morgan, she had reported, seemed almost obsessively interested in hearing all about Cranford's very early days in Yorkshire. Ambrose, listening, was impelled to tease out any implications. Was it just curiosity, he wondered as Vickie rang off, or had there been a crossing of paths years ago that might be casting a shadow in the present? Cranford himself had proved evasive on family origins. Perhaps this was where the paths had crossed. Of course one needed some hard facts, but if there was an American overlap to the story, as was very possible, any family links could readily be explored on M.I.T.'s billion-dollar computer, which devoured family records from all directions.

It was, of course, a flimsy idea at this stage, but what harm would there be in pursuing it? He looked at his watch. Getting on for midnight in England, but still lively enough at M.I.T. for those who kept late hours. His old pal George Angelli never left until seven or eight, Massachusetts time.

He picked up the phone and was through in what one could truly call a split second. "Hi, George," he said to his pal. "I've got a little problem for you. You're going to like it. I think we might use that awful word and call it a challenge."

7

SLEEPING LATE THE next day, Vickie found, over her orange juice, toast, and coffee, that Lord Cranford's arts festival had suddenly become, as it were, an official establishment subject. Until then, it had existed within Suffolk limits, known only to aficionados of festivals and friends of the Ashenham Cricket Club. Now it was being featured, with the new verbosity of *The Times,* in the copy she had picked up at her door. For what must have seemed to them good journalistic reasons, they had gone to town on it.

Ever since *The Times* had given up its old beautifully dry style in reporting the news and begun to offer readers prolix features on feminism and the pop world in the new style of the *Guardian,* they seemed desperate for subjects that could fill the features page garrulously enough. A casual discovery that the Pelham Court Festival was due to open in a week's time gave them the chance they needed. The arts page would have thought it enough to offer a few factual notes, such as that there would be an exhibition of pottery by the Japanese Hokimodo, and a performance of Opus 135 by the Guarneri Quartette, but for the features page one had to stimulate a little sensationalism. This was the first festival in the series that Lord Cranford, the new owner of Pelham Court, was undertaking, and this surely would offer a security challenge to Scotland Yard. Lord Cranford had already received one bomb threat from—it was thought—a splinter Irish terrorist organization and might reasonably expect a renewal of the danger. The Suffolk police, being interviewed, said that they saw no special danger; would Scotland Yard leave things like this?

There was a little supportive sensationalism, too, in digging out the participants in the theatrical show this year. A large picture of the handsome Lady Cranford, the actress Margaretta Paradiso, was accompanied by one of the Irish actor Patrick Hearn, with the news that the play, based on a famous French novel dealing with the degeneracy of the upper classes, was being presented in an Irish setting, which was surely rather suggestive. All in all, it was a typical long-drawn-out *Times* feature page piece in which they might well have scooped the *Guardian* for once.

In his delightful Suffolk cottage, George Sekelis, giving *The Times* twenty minutes of close reading, as he did every morning for items (especially in obituaries, salesroom prices, and the Personal column) that might yield something profitable for the world of antiques, was very satisfied at the fillip this festival article was likely to give to sales at his shop, but rather disturbed to see the security aspect so heavily emphasized. He had talked to Pierre the day before to see if it was still the view that the man chosen should be sent in to get at the archives while Lord Cranford was attending his wife's play. It still seemed good tactics, Pierre said. A break-in at Pelham Court was "safe" in the sense that it would look like a normal country-house burglary, with no overtones for them. Subject to conditions at the time, the man should go ahead.

A hundred and sixty miles south of the Suffolk setting, Rhodine and Emilia, chatting about the *Times* piece over breakfast, saw nothing in it that affected *their* world, being more concerned, in fact, with the mysterious telephone call to Rhodine from O'Leary in which he had announced that she could expect an American visitor on

Wednesday, the day that had now arrived. Rhodine had in mind to take whoever it was to the Dog and Duck for a beer and a plate of their famed cold beef. She had no clear idea what the visit was about, having mostly forgotten the goings-on with O'Leary and Sandra in the groovy Harlem club to which they'd taken her. But one should return hospitality, and Americans always liked English pubs. Emilia agreed and would have joined them but was too heavily involved that day at lunchtime with a really serious situation that had developed at Aston's. She had persuaded Warren Faversham, Josephine Trout, and Leo Forrest to meet with her for lunch in a private room at Georgio's in St. Martin's Lane to plan some coordinated action in resisting the terrible Cranford plans for the firm, which were getting clearer every day. It was not just that he would clearly refuse to step aside as chairman in deference to any cash offer, however large, that she might make. Far worse, she was getting the feeling that he might be seeking amalgamation with a huge company in a way that would mean a loss of independence for Aston's. Leo Forrest, very knowledgeable about the murky bypaths of publishing, had suggested that something even more nefarious might be afoot. The company angling for them, with Cranford not resisting them outright, was a very large concern, backed rather mysteriously by American financing. Was it not possible that that this company was a secret Cranford front? He would hand over Aston's to them and then see it reemerge as part of a larger empire at his sole command.

If Vickie had been privy to this discussion, she might have seen a similarity in this to the fate that had overtaken Baxby and Thomson at an early stage in the young Thomson's career. Even without this parallel before them, the Aston directors could see the lines of danger clearly enough. Warren Faversham alone seemed reluctant to get committed to open opposition. He advised caution for a while before trying to devise alternate plans, such as enlisting the help of another small but friendly publishing house to enlarge the Aston base. Emilia wondered, as she had before, what had got into Faversham. He surely had no taste for Cranford's threatening plans, yet seemed to have lost his stomach for a fight.

As always, Emilia dashed off to work first. Rhodine took it more easily and was just emerging from her bath when the phone rang. An American voice said: "Is that Rhodine? This is Billie. Tim told me to ring." It sounded like a girl's voice, but surely . . . "I've just got in," the caller went on. "I hope you're going to ask me to lunch. You are? Around one? Great! I have to have my hair done this morning. It's a real mess. Can you tell me . . . Luigi? Just across the road from your office? I sure will mention your name. And Roop too. Yeah, everyone knows Roop. Hope I can see him again. Okay. Till one." Rhodine was still gasping. Should she have expected that Billie might be a girl? Only on the principle that everything in America is designed to surprise you. All she could remember from that night on New York was that when she mentioned to O'Leary that a bomb had already been sent to Lord Cranford, he and the horrible Stogie had exchanged looks, with one of them saying: "Sounds like a job for Billie." Time had dissipated the rest of the Harlem picture for Rhodine, though not, it seemed, for O'Leary.

A Billie arrived as promised, if in strange guise, at nearly one. She looked under thirty, with long blond hair falling loosely over her shoulders and dressed in the most chic kind of casual clothes—a pink blouse tucked into beautifully cut red slacks, with a short leather jacket hanging loosely over all. She was obviously enjoying Rhodine's continuing bewilderment. "You expected

138

some he-man?'' she said, grinning impishly. ''Never fails. I get it all the time.''

She was looking round the room with lively pleasure, nodding approvingly at some of Rhodine's drawings mounted on a canvas screen—''Hey! That's neat! I like that!''—and taking in the assorted bric-a-brac stuck all over the walls, newspaper advertisements, invitations, photograph blowups, picture postcards from the Louvre or the Uffizi brought together cheerfully and with bursts of colour here and there from long hangings of silk or woollen yarns looped casually over bits of sculpture that looked like raidings from Egyptian or Greek tombs. She had taken it all in with joy. ''Gee, Sandra said you were great but I didn't expect this!'' In the same breath she managed to express her delight with Rhodine herself. ''Am *I* glad to have got this assignment,'' she went on. ''We'll have a good time, I think.''

Assignment! Rhodine had still not taken things in. ''Tim told me you'd be visiting,'' she began rather tentatively, ''but didn't say what you were going to do.''

''Well,'' Billie said. ''One doesn't need to spell things out, especially over the phone.'' She looked round, seeming to suggest that the room might be bugged. ''We can talk about it over lunch if you like,'' she said, ''but we don't really have to talk about business, do we? Perhaps you'll show me London a bit. I've been here, but I don't really know it. I met Roop when I was here last time. Love to see him again. What a guy! Is he around, do you think?''

Rhodine was still trying to make sense of things. She couldn't possibly believe what seemed to be building up. Something like crossed wires seemed the obvious explanation. But it was impossible to resist this bubbly girl's good fun. ''Roop's away today,'' she said. ''I happened to hear him saying he was going to Paris. But you can see him when he comes back. How long are you staying?"

"Not sure," Billie said. "Depends a bit on your pal's decision, doesn't it? I've got a bed at a friend's house in Fulham Road. Hate staying at hotels, don't *you?* All that filling in forms and records! I like to come and go when I feel like it." She grinned. "Like a bird, maybe. Do you think I look like a bird?"

Rhodine looked at her. That was just what she *did* look like: airy, volatile, delicious. No—she couldn't be involved in anything so . . . Something had gone wrong, but it didn't really matter. Once they had cleared it away, she was going to enjoy Billie. Wasn't America marvellous! First, that sleek monster Sandra—fabulous. And now this bubbly girl. "How about lunch?" she asked her. "I thought of our local pub, the Dog and Duck, just round the corner from Luigi's. But of course, if you . . ."

"The Dog and Duck! Wonderful. Just what I'd hoped for."

"The only thing," Rhodine murmured, "I don't know if we can talk there."

"Damn sight better than one of those fancy joints where you eat out of your neighbour's lap. Pub's much better. For one thing, they can't bug you there. Too noisy."

Behind the froth, this girl seemed to be drawing on a certain amount of practical experience. Within fifteen minutes they were sitting at a little scrubbed table at the less crowded end of the pub. Not surprisingly, Billie had declined the offer of what was called "real ale" (a speciality of the pub) and opted for a nicely chilled bottle of white wine and a plate of smoked salmon. "It's dreamy," Billie said, giving Rhodine a direct look for the first time, with a lot tucked away behind it.

She had proved right about the chance to talk freely in a crowded pub if you were shed of immediate neighbours. Gradually, as they talked, Rhodine was coming to terms with the fact that Tim O'Leary or his pal Stogie had taken quite seriously the talk of disposing of Lord Cranford. To her own amazement, she found herself even considering for a moment the possibility that Emilia, in her present mood, might actually go along with the idea. What she found really hard to accept, however, was the role of Billie in these affairs. For a little more freedom to talk, they strolled into the Green Park, close by, after the pub lunch. Sitting on a bench, Billie was quite forthcoming on the logic behind the arrangement.

"The FBI are very stupid," she explained. "They concentrate on following people who have to hang around on a free-lance basis to do a few jobs; in our case they never succeed in getting them linked to the job itself. It hasn't occurred to them that someone unexpected, like me, might just be on the spot with no apparent connection to the people they've been following, but quite capable of handling the job if that's what's needed."

Rhodine looked at her with continuing astonishment but not total disbelief. "You mean it's really you who would have to do this job?"

Billie shook her pretty head demurely. "I would never actually talk about this, even to a friend like you. But I'll just mention one thing. I was in Amsterdam a week ago. Tim had been there, with the FBI following him. He left, and I stayed on. If anything happened there—and something *did* happen there—I was available."

"Are there others like you?" Rhodine asked, trying desperately to cling to reality in a would-be matter-of-fact way. "How are the jobs distributed? Why are *you* particularly here now?"

"It was the mention of a bomb," Billie said. "Stogie seemed to think that that might turn out to be the best way in this case, and they know I'm rather good at it. I come from Montana and went to the Montana College of Mining, where we learned all about handling dynamite.''

''And what are your plans?'' Rhodine asked, still trying to be calm about it all.

''I'm going to look around,'' Billie said. ''Did you see an article in this morning's *Times* about an arts festival that's going to be held at the end of next week at Lord Cranford's country house? I thought I'd go up there beforehand to look it over just in case. I'm told that there's a very attractive abbey nearby with lots of turrets and gargoyles that American tourists go to, so I'll pop along there, perhaps.''

''Don't you want to see Emilia first? After all . . .''

''You think she may have cold feet? I need to speak to Tim first, anyhow. We could meet for a drink when I get back from the country, say Tuesday at six. Plenty of time. What are you doing tonight?''

Just before noon that day Felix Morgan had found his way to a telephone booth near the UEI building, and looked into his wallet for a short list of telephone call-box numbers that he kept there. It was just a chance, but it usually worked for them when they both felt that a word might help. Noon was a favoured time. He dialed the number of the call-box near the Pelham Arms. The tall dark woman was in the booth and picked up the phone after the third ring.

''Hi!'' he said. ''I thought you might be around. I suppose you saw the article in *The Times*. They're going to be looking for trouble there.''

''I know,'' she murmured. ''Are you sure you want to go ahead? You know, I'm getting a bit afraid.''

''Was anything said to you this morning about the article?''

''No, nothing that matters. Are you sure it will be all right? I must tell you, now that it's getting so near, that I feel—well, a bit different about the whole thing. And now this article. I wondered if you felt something different now. You don't, I think."

"It's been planned," he said. "If other things come up, one still has to go on."

But there was a note of uncertainty in the air on both sides as they put the receivers down.

Inspector Green and Sergeant Brougham had had a quick word about the article that morning, and after going round the subject in general terms, the inspector had unexpectedly come forward with what his sergeant thought a splendid idea.

"How would you like to station yourself up there next week while the festival is taking shape?" he said. "Never mind cultural anthropology this time; just wander anywhere you like among the locals, and the performers, and the tourists in the neighbourhood. You may pick up something in this early phase of the preparations, and we can tighten arrangements later. I suppose you could stay at your people's place, and just be on holiday, as it were. Plain clothes and all that."

Anthony was delighted. "No anthropology, I promise. I've got a better takeoff point: I'll get in some cricket practice."

"*Cricket!*"

"Yes. The village plays Lazenby for a special one-day match during the festival on the Saturday; a short match, just forty overs, so as to end by six, to fit in with the evening performances. They want me to play, of course. I used to play a bit for Oxford, but I'm rusty, and a little practice will do me good."

"A little police-work practice would do you more good," the inspector said. But there was a slight twinkle in his eye. He really quite liked this ridiculous sergeant who'd been foisted on him by the higher-ups at the Yard for a bit of old Green's experience on the way up the ladder. *Cricket practice!* Ah well. It wasn't at all a bad cover in that part of the world.

Ambrose had read the *Times* story over breakfast, and thought about it quite a lot. Strange that *The Times* had perhaps got to the heart of things through a gossip feature, without any hint of what might surface through Vickie's safari in Yorkshire. It was now 8 A.M., and he was sitting in his room waiting for a call from America in response to his call the night before.

Eight A.M. at Oxford—3 A.M. at M.I.T. in Cambridge, Mass. A little midnight oil, and they would now be ready. Sure enough, the phone rang just then, with George Angelli on the line.

"It's okay," George said. "We've managed to re-arrange things. ILSE is waiting."

"I love ILSE," Ambrose said, "though I won't be playing the games she likes. No Infra-Logical Structure Experiments this time. Just a free-for-all informational jag for once."

"That's often more trouble," his friend said. "When will you come?"

"I'll take the morning plane; should be with you around five if the plane's on time. You can start on some of the things I mentioned, including army service pictures if they're available."

"Already in hand. Be seeing you."

8

ANTHONY HAD TAKEN his police duties seriously enough to mingle with the visitors to Lyddiham Abbey on the Monday before the festival. The reward was prompt. A gorgeous American girl called Billie was among the tourists. "Do you like antiques?" he said to her as they came out of the grounds together. "I have a friend in the village who has a shop with nice things. He's a Bulgarian called Sekelis. All the tourists go there."

"Sounds like a clip-joint. I'll skip it for the moment," Billie said in the brisk style that he was beginning to find enchanting. He had caught sight of this long-legged blonde only an hour earlier, standing out very clearly among the others, inspecting the strange structures of the abbey from the outside before starting the regulation tour within of the twelfth-century arches and the effigies. He had attached himself, since she seemed as willing as he was to make the most of the encounter.

"I live fairly near here, or at least my parents do," he explained. "I'm taking a break from London. I'd love to show you round, some very pretty villages. Is there anything you particularly want to see?"

They were wandering along the High Street and had reached her car, parked near a small cluster of shops, one of which proudly offered Suffolk Teas. "Do you feel like tea? It's nearly four o'clock, our regulation time."

"Aren't you nice," she said, "taking care of me like this. Truth is I'd rather wait till the pubs open. Isn't it crazy? You have to wait till six or something to get a drink. Tell you what, if you're free for an hour or so. I read an article in *The Times* last week about a big arts festival coming up, so I thought I'd drive up ahead of time and find a place to stay and then go to what appealed to me. The house itself where the festival's held is supposed to be quite something, according to the article. Is it nice painting country? Oh, it must be—Constable and all that. I do quite a lot of painting myself and brought my oils with me. I suppose you know where the place is. Do they mind people putting up an easel?"

"They'd love it," Anthony said enthusiastically. What a girl, he thought. Those legs, and now a painter, too. "I know the house, and I'm quite sure they won't mind you installing yourself for a bit of painting. I'm quite free if you want to go now. It's only about fifteen minutes' drive out there, and you can look around."

"Oh, great!" she cried. "Jump in. Sorry for the mess." It was a small Ford. The space behind the front seats was cluttered with bags and a large painting box. "My easel and stool are in the boot," she said. "I rented the car. Crazy small but goes real fast along these narrow roads, or anyhow it seems like it."

There was a man in leggings, obviously part of the estate staff, at the lodge gates. Anthony wondered if someone from A. T. was keeping an eye on things more discreetly.

The man was grumpy but quite acquiescent when they waited in the car to see if it was okay for them to drive through. If he recognized Anthony, he didn't say anything. One had the impression that Pelham Court was fully open, and would stay open to everybody, including a potential bomber, despite the warnings in *The Times* on security. Billie was taking it all in with the wide-eyed innocence that was now familiar to him.

"Gosh, it's enormous," she said, as they drove along the curving road, with a glimpse of the house in what seemed like the far distance. "All these grounds and cottages, and those little structures—what are they?"

"They call them follies."

"Isn't that just right?" she said with delight. "Perhaps they used them to lock up naughty girls who'd misbehaved when their husbands were away fighting the Crusades. Have I got the history right?"

"Absolutely," he said, "except that *we* were brought up to believe that the girls were put into dungeons. I can just see you there. You'd be a natural with those blond locks . . ."

"And you'd come and rescue me."

"You bet. Look over there to the left. That's the Great Barn where the performances take place. It's Elizabethan, and the longest barn in England."

"Could we drive over to see it?"

"Certainly. Just take that road."

It seemed obvious as they got nearer why at this stage there was such a perfunctory guard at the gate. The barn was thronged with workmen—or artists dressed up to look like workmen—busy in every field, from dealing with small things like shelves, curtains, chairs, doorways, and lights, to some major projects on the stage, where much was going on in fixing screens that turned or opened. There was not much point, it seemed to Anthony, in holding up this heterogeneous throng under controls set up at the distant lodge gates. Yet security surely demanded it. It was a point he would have to raise later with the inspector. In the meantime they got out to wander over the scene with no restraint, strolling off, also, from the barn to the meadows nearby to see the house itself from another angle.

"Where do you think you might paint?" he asked her. "Do you like those sheep near the stream? If you put in a shepherdess you'd have a real Constable."

"Could we look around the outside of the house itself?" she asked. "I'd really like to sit down here and there to find a good subject."

The great front view, with its porticoes and rows of windows looking down to a vast array of ordered lawns didn't appeal. "What about the back, the old part over there?" she asked. "I suppose this is the servants' entrance. Oh, that corner, near that old door. I could stand there and look out toward that separate little house. It's a really nice composition. You don't think I'll have to get special permission? If I start painting, I might be here half the day."

At that moment, a gnarled old man came out of the door of a nearby cottage and began walking towards them. "I know him," Anthony murmured to her. "He's George Knowles, been here all his life. I used to see him when I came over with my father to see the former owner, Lord Tenderden. I wonder if he'll remember me."

"Why, it's Mr. Anthony," the old boy croaked, with the vowel in "why" given a full Suffolk accent. "You've come to see me, eh? How's your father? And who's this pretty young girl you've brought to show me? Must be your lady. Very pleased to see you, Miss."

"She's a painter," Anthony said. "Would it be all right for her to bring her paints over tomorrow?"

The old boy gave a wheezy laugh. "Be wanting to paint me, I daresay, in my old shooting coat, my father's coat, I mean. You just come here and paint, my dear, whether I'm here or not. May not be here tomorrow, but don't let that trouble you."

He tottered off, and they got into the car for the drive back to Ashenham. "I'll tell you something," Anthony said, "now that you've been admitted to the charmed circle. If you want to come in and I'm not around, you don't have to go through the lodge gates. They might just be closed. But there's another way in through a small side road about half a mile away. You can use it with no trouble. There's just an ordinary gate in the hedge to keep the cows in. Be sure to close it when you've gone through. We can go that way now. I'll guide you.''

Back in Ashenham, they made their way to a little restaurant, Le Provencal, which had opened the year before to cater to the tourist trade with food that added a continental touch to plain old Suffolk. Perhaps George Sekelis had had a hand in getting it started—perhaps he even owned it. One never knew with George, Anthony thought. He had heard a lot in the restaurant's praise but never been there. Here was the ideal chance, in the company of this glorious girl.

It was a mile outside the village, arty in the new English-European style, with wurst, onions and garlic hanging everywhere in profusion and a phoneydom of foreign accents as they were welcomed by the manager and waiters. However, they were soon *à table,* with a glass of white wine before them, and a massive menu with every dish-name, in French and English, smothered in a revolting over-plus of description. It was when they were finally launched into the meal that an extra piquant touch made its appearance.

Billie had got round to asking Anthony what his job was in London. "I'm a policeman," he said.

"A policeman!" Her big blue eyes opened up wider and wider. "A policeman!" There was nothing else that she could bring herself to say. This nice young man, such a charmer, with his tousled hair and showing her everything she had come to look at, was a policeman. What would Tim say when he heard?

On his side, it simply never occurred to Anthony that he might tell Inspector Green of his conquest. No point, really, when it clearly had nothing to do with his job.

* * *

Inspector Green, as it happened, had gone that morning to see the assistant commissioner whose area of responsibility covered Anti-Terrorism. They had begun with a brief word about administrative arrangements during the superintendent's continued absence. Nothing specific was said about the time this was taking, but the inspector thought he detected a hint that this might have repercussions for himself on the career front. Had they finally decided to move him up to the post? It would fit from many angles. He nursed the thought with great satisfaction.

At the practical level, the assistant commissioner's main concern in their talk was the threat in the IRA's sudden announcement that day that they were going to extend their violence once again to the mainland. The inspector gave him a detailed account of occasions and localities that seemed likely to offer the drama that the IRA needed, supplementing the obvious and grimly familiar settings—bombings of members of Parliament, army barracks, and so on—on which they had long established a frightening position. "What about this big arts festival in Suffolk that I read about in *The Times* last week?" the assistant commissioner asked. "It must certainly be tempting for them," the inspector said, "to try to cash in on the Cranford story, though it's a month since it happened. The letter-bomb sent to him wasn't claimed by the IRA and didn't quite bear their signature, but there's nothing to stop them picking it up."

"How irritating of *The Times* to revive the story now," the assistant commissioner said. "Typical of the media: always trying to make things harder for us. Still, we have to deal with it. Can you tell me what special arrangements you've made?"

"The festival itself is a scattered collection of events, but a lot goes on in a very big barn, which we're protecting from all possible angles, of course. On the more

150

general front, I sent up one of my sergeants who knows the area very well to have a good look round, especially in relation to Lord Cranford's house, which has got to be a prime target in any IRA bomb campaign. He'll be dealing with access to the grounds, and ways of getting into the house itself that avoid the usual alarms. I'm sure we can count on him. He's a rather unusual sergeant. You probably know about him, Anthony Brougham, son of Viscount Calshott, who lives near there.''

"Oh, yes. I remember him. We just moved him to you. How's he doing?''

"I wouldn't say he's a born policeman in the traditional sense, though he got good reports as a constable on the beat, and during a spell on fraud. He's certainly very likeable, and he's also very imaginative. A little too much, perhaps, sometimes. But on this festival caper, I thought he would be perfect. Knows the area very well. Actually plays cricket for the local team. He certainly won't let anything unusual get past him. I'm playing the whole thing in tandem. Two regular A. T. men and two women constables have gone up there as a separate team reporting in the first place to the Suffolk police. But Brougham is on his own, in touch with Suffolk, of course, but reporting straight to me if he spots anything that might have a bearing on A. T. business generally. I'm sure we can count on him. He's a very conscientious officer.''

For some time now, Vickie had been establishing a regular pattern of research in the Chesham Square archives, with only short breaks during working hours for a sandwich and a drink at the wine-bar opposite Justin de Blank's shop on Elizabeth Street. But if the work was becoming routine, something of a very different character had invaded her personal life, and never left her mind for a moment.

151

On the first day after the Yorkshire journey she had worked without interruption, with dinner agreed for the evening with Felix Morgan. He had called for her at her Westminster flat and driven her to a new place he had found for her, as he put it: a little candle-lit Italian restaurant in a back street off Paulton's Square, mercifully free of the noisy hustle that is thought, in Chelsea, to go naturally with Chianti and pasta. In Felix's new place, by contrast, the owner and his comfortably buxom wife generated an air of quiet friendship, as if the setting was a little Tuscan village, with the guests joining the family and a few friends. Responding to this, the talk, after they had settled down at a nice corner table, was rather gentle and happy, drifting away at times into gasps of pleasure on the food and wine, but often leaving them content, it seemed, just to enjoy each other's presence. When Felix drove her home, it felt natural that he went up with her and put his arm around her as they stood for a while looking out on the Westminster skyline, with the Abbey solemn and timeless under the scudding clouds. It was natural, too, that they moved into her bedroom and embraced with passion and tenderness.

At peace afterward, she felt that something hard in her life had given way at last. He too, she sensed, had been freed in a transforming way. She had no idea what it meant for him, but she felt it.

He had told her that he was going away on business with Cranford for the next two days to look at some factories in Sweden. She had been rather glad to be left on her own, burying herself in the archives but feeling free and happy in a new way, without needing to put it into any kind of positive framework.

The work itself was going well, and it was good to think that he might be ringing her that night whether he was back or still away. The phone rang indeed as she came through the door at around 6:30, but it was Ambrose.

"Hallo," she began cheerfully, but his tone in reply was rather brusque. "Are you on your own?" he asked. And when she said she was, he went on: "Something sensational has happened, and I have to talk to you very urgently. It affects you very directly. You started something, and I've taken it further, and now there's a chance that you might be able to come up with the missing pieces. You're not going to like it, but we have to try."

"What are you talking about?" she cried. "What has happened?"

"Nothing yet, and we have to try and stop what *could* happen. Something odd has grown up around you, a bomb sent to Cranford, a mystery around his origins, and other things. Yorkshire's in the middle of it because Cranford has put Yorkshire on like a mask, and he may be fooling us. Do you remember the theme of *Moby Dick?* 'Break through the mask!' When you told me about Shilton, I felt that Cranford didn't want us to find out where he came from, which made it very important for us *to* find out. The best way is through family relationships. It's a hard nut to crack in a short time, but we can tackle it in a double-barreled way: I can pursue one line, you another. I don't know what we'll come up with, but I decided to start things going anyhow, off my own bat. And something startling has already shown up."

"You mean on family matters that might have some serious meaning?"

"Exactly. And you do understand: this is strictly between the two of us for the moment."

"Oh, I'll agree to that. But what have you worked on? Are you phoning from Oxford?"

"I'm phoning from America."

She had to repeat it in a dumbfounded way: *"America! When did you go there?"* And as she said it, she knew instinctively that it affected Felix, and that it was he in particular who hadn't to be told.

"I came over yesterday because of the two elements in the story. You're focussed on the English end; *I* wanted to look at the same characters from the American end. There's a marvellous way into this for me: the M.I.T. computer that I told you about. I have a friend there who got them to give me some working time. My ordinary programme is on the logic of language, but I wanted to use it differently: to absorb and analyze the vast quantities of information now available on all aspects of the U.S. population. I expect you know that this is all computerized here more than in any other country of the world. They call the machine ILSE—initials for what it does on the logical programme—but it's marvellous to see it handling the personal stuff about the U.S. population, which includes, of course, origins and relationships into which you can cut with the flick of a switch. Naturally, that's what I'm after. When you told me about your Yorkshire visit, I decided to see what would happen if we fed ILSE with all the U.S. family names that hinge on the Cranford story, and see if any led to Yorkshire, and if so, where?"

"And if any had some link to Cranford's bomb," Vickie said slowly, her heart sinking. "And you wanted it immediately, instant analysis, I suppose."

"That's just it," Ambrose said sombrely. "This wasn't something to hang around for a history book to discover. *The Times* may have got it right. If there was one bomb as a warning, what about another for real impact at the festival? We need a firm family link to emerge, and a second one for corroboration. ILSE's been rushing through thousands of names and places and family relationships to see if anything jells. It's just incredible to see how she follows all the details and picks out anything that's been specified."

154

"And a link has come through?"

"A *possibility* has come through, and that's what I want you to work on, at speed. If there is a bomb lined up and you can find out what's behind it, we could get the whole background documented, and then confront those concerned."

Vickie was taking it all in, more miserable by the second. "It's Felix, isn't it? He's in the middle of it all? I noticed how you reacted when I told you how interested he is in my work on the archives. He's trying to find out about Cranford's origins, just as I am."

"Oh, my poor Vickie," Ambrose said. "I wish it was that, but it's worse. As I see it, you've got it upside down. He's not trying to find out. He *knows,* and he wants to make sure that you don't. He's in the middle all right, and you've got to find out what it means. He defused the first bomb, or gave the impression. He may not be so helpful with a second one."

"But how could I find out, all on my own . . ."

Ambrose interrupted. "Wait till I tell you what I think is behind all this, and what's suddenly emerged as a clue. For you to be able to build on it will be a long shot, but we've got to try it. If it stops what's being planned, it would be worth it. It's the only way we might be able to pin the story together. Listen. Can you go off to Yorkshire tonight, without any awkward questions being asked? You do see that I have to ask this because of Morgan."

"Yes, it could all make sense if he's part of the Yorkshire connection. I don't want to believe it, but yes, it could be. I admit it. What do I have to do?"

"First thing is not to answer any more phone calls tonight. Then your car. Is it in good shape for a long journey? It is? Good. Now the drive. I want you to pack a toothbrush and a notebook and drive to Yorkshire tonight, so that you can be ready to start the job first thing in the morning. My guess is that the drive shouldn't take you more than seven or eight hours on the motorway at night, allowing for a break for food on the way. You may need the car there or I'd say go by train.''

''Where am I going to in Yorkshire? To Shilton again?''

''No, to Longbeck, a little coal-mining town far to the north, on the border of Durham. It's good that you can go tonight. Time's so short before the festival. Every hour could count.''

''Yes, I'll go, and not a word to anyone. But for God's sake tell me what you've worked out so far, and where this place Longbeck comes into the story.''

''I'm going to be very brief,'' Ambrose said, ''because I'm sure you've had some of the same ideas yourself. Cranford's origin is the starting point. When facts are scarce one has to jump into a theory and then test it against things one *does* know. We both have what one might call a working theory that he must have a special reason for not mentioning his birthplace in his very long entry in *Who's Who*. He could have identified himself and also given the place a little fame. But he left it out. It seemed to you as if he wanted to wipe the place out of the record, and if so, this was significant.

''What can we tack onto that? Morgan keeps asking— I suppose discreetly, but quite persistently—whether anything on Cranford's very early days has surfaced in the archives. You think this means he's curious; *I* think it means he's afraid. I just don't believe that Morgan has worked for Cranford all this time without finding out anything he wanted to know about him. So I try on a theory for size. He's afraid that if you find out something about Cranford's very early days and it shows some link to Morgan himself, it may bring out something that he, Morgan, wants to keep dark. So he keeps close track of you. Are you in fact on the verge of stumbling on the facts? So far you don't seem to be, which is why we have to get to work. Between us we may get there by a different method, my double-barreled way, me on ILSE and you in Yorkshire."

"And you've done your side? The machine's come through?"

"We've at last got a hard nugget out of ILSE, very hard. I'll spare you all the false leads we've had, but now we've really got a Yorkshire connection, which is why I rang you. And there are some signs of more to come, once they've cleared away any possible mixup in names. What's come through already is positive, but with a hole in the middle. The hole is what you've got to fill in on the ground."

"What's the positive part?"

"You'd better prepare yourself for a shock, though perhaps you've guessed. It's on Morgan's origins. According to ILSE, his father, Joseph Morgan, was born in Yorkshire, in the place I've mentioned: Longbeck. He migrated to Canada in 1929 or 1930 from England with his wife, who was also born in Longbeck. Her maiden name was Lucy Mandell. We can't be sure yet about the details, but I think they moved from Canada to Chicago not long afterward. They were naturalized as U.S. citizens in 1935. When the data gets firmer, it lists six children, one called Felix." He broke off. "Wait a minute. The stuff we were hoping for has been cleared, so there's more coming in. Don't ring off."

Vickie sat there waiting. It would be about Margaretta, she was sure. She had come into the Cranford story through Cranford's Chicago friend Masolino. The Chicago connection. From the other end she heard muffled voices, and Ambrose was suddenly back.

"It's amazing. Now that ILSE has got going, we can't stop her."

"It's about Margaretta, isn't it?"

"That was my thought, too, and we're right. Her father was born in Italy, migrated to the U.S.A. in 1926 and married his wife there in 1931. She was born in Long-beck, maiden name Maria Mandell. They're listed with five children, one called Margaretta."

"So she and Felix are probably cousins," Vickie said, "but for some reason no one mentions it. It really is very strange. And is there any mention of Herbert Thomson being linked to this Yorkshire town, Longbeck?"

"No mention at all. That's the hole you've got to fill. I'm sure there's a link; there's got to be. And you'll find it."

"You think things will just open up in Longbeck, given what's come out so far? You see it as a firm base?"

Ambrose laughed. "Firm base? Absolutely not. What we've got are a few bare bones for Longbeck; tremendously interesting, but without any real sign of how they're to be put together. All I can tell you firmly is to count on Usher's Law of the Unexpected: if the facts so far seem to be pointing in one direction, you can be sure that things will end up differently."

"You're making my job easier and easier, aren't you? Do you have any firm information at least on Longbeck itself?"

"Ah, there I can help you. ILSE is very good on topography. Apparently Longbeck is—or rather, was—a quite substantial coal-mining town in North Yorkshire, near the border with Durham, as I said. Once produced a lot of coal; shrank during the coal troubles of the 1920s, but still had about fifty thousand population, and was obviously a tight-knit community socially, like all those northern coal towns. Today, the population has shrunk, with the closing of most of the coal-mines, but it's probably a busy little place still. In the early days, side by side with coal, there's a mention of small factories and workshops. It's amazing what ILSE trundles out if

158

you just ask her for facts, without expecting her to add things up. I expect they made metal goods for the pit workings and other basic needs, running repairs and all that. Nothing very distinguished in all this, except in one regard.''

"And I can guess what that was," Vickie said, fresh from her reading about northern social life. "They had a good football team.''

"You're a marvel," Ambrose said. "Yes, one of those great old teams that stays in the town's record forever as a shining jewel of a fact, which ILSE ferrets out with ease. Longbeck was in the first division of the Football League for quite a time, and on one occasion reached the Cup Final at Wembley. It was in 1928. They didn't win the cup, but they got to Wembley.''

"Oh, good," Vickie said. "That's given me a sense of reality for the first time." She was suddenly cheerful about the whole project. "Maybe I'll track down Thomson, and we'll see that it's all a nightmare. I'll have to go anyhow.''

"It's speed that's the problem," Ambrose said. "You could track down all the records if there was time, but we don't have time. Let's stop now and talk tomorrow night to see if anything is beginning to emerge. Ring me at any time, collect. Here's how to reach me.'' He gave her the number at M.I.T. and the name of the colleague who could also accept the collect call. "And here's my hotel number and room. I think that's all, and we should stop. I don't want to delay things in case someone comes round to see you before you get away. So let's say goodbye now, and good luck.''

"Thanks," she said ruefully, as she put the phone down. Within a minute it rang again. She was sure who it was and let it go on ringing. It stopped, and then began again ten minutes later. It continued to ring as she left the flat with an overnight bag in her hand.

159

She had expected it to be a nightmare journey, but in the event going by road fitted well into the character of what lay ahead. It was a journey through oblivion into a state where an entirely new situation might be born. En route one crossed the Styx, reconciled to accepting whatever Fate might bring, in a mysterious confrontation with reality.

The road was carrying little traffic, but the huge trucks that overtook her from time to time at something like ninety miles an hour called for an act of concentration that drove out useless thought on what might be emerging from this doubtful unravelling of the past. Keeping one's mind on the road solved most of the immediate problem; music was the other solvent. A tape of the *St. Matthew Passion* was complemented perfectly, after fifteen minutes of silence, by *Porgy and Bess*. For a much-needed rest, she stopped off at a motorway café near Nottingham to deal with a ghastly hamburger and some restorative coffee. The *AA Handbook* gave her the number of the Station Hotel at Longbeck, where she secured a room, saying she would arrive at around 2 A.M. She was pretty tired when she arrived, but a double whiskey helped. She asked to be called at 8 A.M., ready to start work at nine.

Sergeant Anthony Brougham had gone to bed in a more seraphic mood that night. Awake next morning in his familiar room at Tesserel Place, he let his mind wander happily at the thought of seeing Billie again. Goodness, he didn't even know her full name, but what did it matter? "Billie" suited her so well. She had been quite encouraging when she gave him a lift back from Le Provençal to where his car was parked near the Ashenham village green. "We won't meet in the morning," she had said. "I'm going to drive out to Pelham Court and really get down to painting that spot I've chosen. It's great that you arranged it all for me, with the private way in and all that. Perhaps we could meet later in the day, say for tea at four at that nice tea-shop."

"That would be great," Anthony said. "I'll be here in the afternoon getting some cricket practice on the green. I'm playing for the village team in the festival match."

"Cricket! You can tell me all about it. It's like baseball, isn't it? You'd better give me your phone number in case I want to get in touch."

"Here it is," he said, scribbling it down with the family name on a bit of paper he tore from a notebook.

Something nice to look forward to. He took his time getting ready for the none-too-heavy duties that lay ahead: an exchange of courtesies with the Suffolk police to talk about security over the festival period, a call to Inspector Green to indicate that he was on the job even if there was nothing to report. As there was time, he thought he would limber up for the cricket. Towel in hand, he wandered over to the pool his father had installed, and did a long stretch, up and down for twenty lengths, before recuperating with a breakfast of kippers and coffee.

Billie, coming into town en route to her morning's work at Pelham Court, had no real thought of tea with Anthony at four since she was already committed, rather more importantly, to meeting Emilia and Rhodine that evening for a drink at the Reform Club, to go into the question of the job that lay ahead. No problem on the job itself, now that she had access and could make her preparations. She hoped that Emilia was going to tell her how to set a time when Cranford was alone in the house, with everybody else at the festival. Always nice to keep the body count down if you could. Of course Emilia might be awkward in a different way. She sounded like one of those people who like things spelt out in something like a real contract. She might be surprised to find that the job could go ahead without any money changing hands in advance, though if she thought about it for a moment she would realise how this could happen. Once a job was launched, there was never a question of the client bowing out without paying. Even if the job was called off, there was what Tim called his "consultation fee." Once Tim's operator had reported for duty, there was no question of the client going to the police to complain. The police would ask too many questions on how it was that O'Leary had set up the deal. A client would have to be out of his or her mind to refuse to pay the consultation fee—in used notes, of course. That, at any rate, was how things like this were organized in the U.S.A., and the same principles surely applied everywhere.

The morning's visit to Pelham Court was quite delightful. Having set up her easel and put a few broad slaps of paint on the canvas, she spent an hour or so looking over the disposition of the walls, doors, and windows of the area she'd decided on, and making a few decisions. At this point, she had a cup of coffee from the vacuum flask she'd brought with her, and then settled down to paint the scene for the fun of it. Later, she would obliterate it to avoid any identification, but it was a good feeling in itself.

At about twelve she drove back to Ashenham, en route to London, and stopped off in the village to visit the antiques shop that Tony had mentioned, owned by his friend—a Bulgarian, he had said. It would do no harm, she thought, to see what the Bulgarian thought about the policeman side of Tony, or anything else that might be useful one day.

Mr. Sekelis, the Bulgarian, was, as she had expected, all charm and flattery. "How like Tony to have such a beautiful friend," he said. "These aristocrats always

162

have exquisite taste. How else would I have such beautiful things from their houses for sale?''

"Why do you say aristocrats?" she asked. "He told me he was a policeman."

"The roles can be combined," Sekelis said. "At least they can in England. It's the secret formula for preserving British society, you know. Leadership by those born to it. Not all are willing to play, but for those that do, like Tony, it's very rewarding. Oh yes, a real aristocrat is Tony. His father is the 11th Viscount Calshott.''

"A *lord!* Does that make Tony a lord, too?"

"Well, it can happen. He's the second son, so there are a few barriers to the title, but they could disappear."

"I remember!" Billie exclaimed. "Like that wonderful movie with Alec Guinness, *Kind Hearts and Coronets.* I've seen it several times on late-night TV. Absolutely great! He had to bump off all kinds of people and then the title was his."

"Well, there you are," Sekelis said. "If you're going to set your cap at Tony, all you have to do is to import a nice agreeable gangster from America to remove the obstacles, and you become Viscountess Calshott. Let's see. There's his father, the present Viscount; his older brother; and any unfortunate sons that the older brother may have. Child's play for Americans."

"Until then, Tony is an aristocrat, but without a title?"

"He *has* a title. He's called *Hon.*, which stands for the Honourable."

"But I don't get that if I marry him?"

"Not really."

"Then we'll have to get rid of the obstacles," Billie said cheerfully as she moved to the door. "I'm going to get right down to it as soon as I can."

He had the door open for her with the most courtly of bows. "So happy to have met you. You're coming to the festival, I hope."

"It's right at the centre of my programme," she said, "especially now that I'm going to become a lady."

* * *

Not everybody was as carefree as Billie. Anthony himself, dressed becomingly in his white cricketing flannels, had spent a rather irritated half-hour waiting for her outside the Suffolk Tea-Shop, where she had more or less promised to meet him. Perhaps she had got too involved with her painting; more honestly he could admit to himself that he really knew nothing of her real interests. She had said very little about herself, though meeting a policeman obviously fascinated her.

It had come out particularly when they had talked over dinner about TV programmes. She had heard that *Miami Vice*, her favourite TV thriller, was now the rage here too. He simply had to see it, especially as a policeman. A misty look had come into her eyes when she began to extol the peculiar excitement of Miami. She went there a lot, partly to visit her grandmother, who lived in Palm Beach, but more to see her friends among the police and on the other side. That was the joy of *Miami Vice*. You didn't have to say which side you were on. Police, private eyes, and "ordinary" people like herself mixed it together with no holds barred. It was really exciting, the things you could get up to in Miami, even as a girl. She had got to know the people who made the *Miami Vice* programme, and would introduce him if he came out. There were direct planes from London now. They would be tickled to death to meet a real live English policeman, might even offer him a part in one of the episodes. He could be a private-eye guardian of a visiting English millionaire on a fishing trip. "We call them 'minders' in England," he said. "We have a wonderful TV programme . . ." and the talk had gone on, happily, cheerfully, but not, it seemed, guiding her next day into the Suffolk tea-shop.

164

Billie had, in fact, arrived in London at about this time and rung O'Leary in New York, using an accommodation number there that was changed daily on a code linked to a page in the *Wall St. Journal* that she carried with her. She had organized the practical side of the job, she told him, but had a feeling that the principal was likely to be very stuffy when they met that evening, unlike her pal who was so up-and-coming. Tim didn't seem too worried. He would be quite prepared to settle for a consultation fee if necessary, and in any case he had something else coming up in a locale she liked that might well need her attention. It was always reassuring to talk to Tim, she thought, as she set about getting dressed for the drink she was to have with Emilia and Rhodine at the Reform Club. A simple little black dress that she was carrying with her seemed just right. All was well.

Felix Morgan had been trying all day to throw off the sense of frustration he had felt the previous evening at not being able to reach Vickie on the telephone. He told himself that he was being unreasonable, but knew at the same time that reason didn't come into it. Of course she could be dining with friends, and in not replying when he telephoned very early in the morning, she might have left even earlier for a swim at the Berkeley Hotel, which she had told him she sometimes did. But no rationalizations really helped. He wanted to see her, to hear her laugh, to say something special to her and hear her response.

There was still no reply when he telephoned in the early evening at six, and then at seven, before setting out to a dinner that Cranford and Margaretta were giving in their home that night to a mixed gathering of businessmen and politicals. At one moment, when all the guests seemed to have arrived and were circulating with drinks in their hands, he found himself standing next to Margaretta, who was keeping a hostess eye on the company but

165

was free to exchange a word with him. Looking at the lively scene, an epitome of his public life, he felt a sudden surge of revulsion at the secret life he had nurtured for so long. He knew even before he spoke that at that moment he was finished with hate and revenge.

"I've given up the plan," he said to her softly.

"For my reasons?"

"No," he said. "I've fallen in love."

Cranford came over at that moment with the Minister of Trade in tow. Margaretta turned to speak to him. She was an actress, her feelings all subdued. Only later, when all the other guests had left and Cranford had gone into his study for a moment with the minister, did she give any sign. A whole life came out in the brief words that she and Felix exchanged.

"It was real," she said to him. "It doesn't just disappear. That time when we found each other, and all the excitement since then."

"It was all wrong," he said. "Even with a new life now, I have a terrible feeling that the shadow may not go away."

"We'll know later," she said. "Give ourselves time . . ."

Cranford came into the room at this point. Felix, getting ready to leave, disappeared for a moment into an adjacent room to make a phone call. No reply.

9

THE TELEPHONE BOOK had to come first, though she knew in advance that the entries would be far too numerous to follow up in a hurry, as it indeed proved. The book showed that the area of which Longbeck was a part, telephonically, had its main centre in a seaside town fifteen miles away called Brayburn, known nationally for an important steelworks close by. The Morgan name had a full page and a half in the directory, roughly five hundred names. Thompson with a "p" was about the same, and though Thomson, as Cranford spelt it, was (to her surprise) much less common, they were still like the sands of the sea, even in Longbeck alone. Mandell or Mandel (she didn't know the spelling) was very thin. She couldn't expect much there. She had equipped herself with a mass of coins from a branch of the Trustee Savings Bank in Newport Road, just in case, but she knew, turning the pages of her directory in the post office next door, that if she was going to find any links, they would have to emerge by themselves, once she had provided a possible springboard to start things off.

Just to make contact with local voices, she did phone and get through to two Morgans and two Thomsons whose addresses specified Longbeck. The only result was, in fact, on the voice side, giving her a chance to take in the local accent, very flat and with none of the Norwegian singsong of the Durham "Geordies," only slightly to the north. The real communication problem lay in trying to break down the inherent suspicion in getting a telephone call from a stranger with a London accent, asking vaguely about old family relatives. She found that she got on best when she spoke about doing a programme on the BBC about the coal industry. Coal and the BBC were two factors in the British scene that people could accept as natural, once the first suspicion was overcome.

She took the telephoning as a kind of prologue, and bent her mind to something which might have firmer content: the town hall. One of the names might mean something to an old-established local official. After a certain amount of shunting, she found herself closeted with a rubicund old gent who was dying to help—one would do anything for the BBC—but produced no link worth following up on any of the names.

Emerging from the town hall and passing the call-box near the door, she had a sudden impulse to try one more telephone call, this time to a Mandell, and for a moment, as she heard the man speaking at the other end, she felt a tinge of excitement. It had worked. She had started with "Excuse me, but could you tell me if you have any family relatives in America, in Chicago, or Los Angeles?"

"Yes," said the man excitedly. "Who is it speaking?"

"I'm collecting information for a programme," Vickie said, "and . . ."

"You mean I've won the prize. I knew I'd win. My wife's grandmother in Kansas . . ."

"Prize?" Vickie said lamely. "What prize . . ."

"The *Daily Express* competition: Hands Across the Sea. I knew no one could beat her grandmother—a full-blooded Cherokee Indian. It had to win. Which of the prizes am I getting?"

Vickie tried desperately to be polite with "We're just checking" as she beat a hasty retreat from the box, feeling distinctly ashamed. Further down the street she saw a large, rather ornate-looking café and made her way there, sinking gratefully into a chair and asking the waitress for coffee. "And biscuits?" "Yes, please," she said.

She had brought a *Yorkshire Post* from the news agent next door, just in case something had developed in the outside world during her excursion into limbo. The headlines gave no such indication. The coffee came from a very modern espresso machine, accompanied by some bourbon biscuits that were immensely comforting. But she was getting nowhere. She hadn't even started. She had to find a new approach that fitted where she was: this café, this town. She signalled for another cup of coffee and looked around her for some sort of inspiration.

The café was certainly unusual, at least to a southerner. It was both plebeian and stylish, the walls in white tiles, lino on the floor, round tables with bentwood period chairs, and on the wall, in coloured tiles, a proud title: "LONGBECK ICE-CREAM PARLOUR, Established 1911." They had broadened this to include "Light Refreshments," as a subsidiary title showed, but the old Ice-Cream Parlour set the tone.

A thought came into her head. An old ice-cream parlour indicated an old family, and this might offer a lead. The waitress, when she came up with the bill, knew nothing to help. "Oh, yes," she said in her rather heavy accent. "But for a long time now, all my life, it's just part of the Brayburn cafés, all over East Yorkshire."

The local tone of her reply acted as a further signpost for Vickie. *The Brayburn Cafés.* They were clearly an institution of the area, and memory was enshrined in institutions. What was the oldest institution? The Football Club. There was no phone in the shop; she could hardly wait to get outside to the call-box near the town hall. Memory would surely be alive in the club, perhaps in the person of a time-worn secretary who had actually been present at the legendary occasion in 1928 when Longbeck didn't win the Cup. There was a telephone number for the ground. The caretaker told her that Mr. Jopping, the Hon. Secretary of the Club, could be found in his office down the Newport Road at the corner of Selby Square. He was a solicitor, Cresley and Jopping. She jumped into her car, and ten minutes later was in his office, enjoying the hospitality that was to prove universal north of Watford, coffee and biscuits, not bourbon in this case, but the more familiar digestive.

Mr. Jopping was about thirty, blunt but chirpy, and anxious to revive any memories that could be projected on the BBC about the grand old club, now consigned, it seemed, to a humble role in a very minor East Yorkshire football league. "Those were the days," he began, preparing to spell out what his grandfather had told him. "No, he died three years ago," he said, when she proposed a direct talk. Of course there was Tom Volkening, over eighty, the keenest old supporter, always to be found from 12:15 onward in a corner chair at the Newport Arms. "A Norwegian name," he volunteered. "Quite a bit of Norwegian influence in these parts. Much stronger, of course, around Newcastle, the real Geordies."

Behind him was a vast cupboard with rows of ledgers: "Minutes, names of players, contracts," he explained. "It would take a very long time to track down all the individual family names. If you're in a hurry, you'd do better to talk to old Tom. He has every name in his head, just like my old grandfather."

Very promising, she thought, but it was still not much after eleven. Jopping, standing up to see her off, stopped for a moment to make another suggestion. "Of course there's Vic Wesley," he said, "at the Miners' Welfare. He's been there forever. Must be nearly ninety by now.

Was a miner, and then worked for a long time in a paid job at the Welfare, and now he just goes in, something to do, and has a pint with sausages and mash for his dinner. I don't know if you'll understand everything he says. He's very lively, it's just our accent, especially the old folk."

"Oh, I'm beginning to get the hang of it," she said as they stood together at the door of her car. She had decided that she had time to go to the Welfare first. Jopping explained the way.

Vic was everything that Jopping promised, ready to wander round every name with reminiscences, all leading nowhere. "I knew a Dick Thomson who played a beautiful cornet in the colliery band, but that's all. Morgan? Now I *do* remember him. That was Jack Morgan who was a mate of mine at the Sowerby pit when I was very young. He was a Catholic, but a nice fellow. Very good cricketer, too. Fast bowler. Yorkshire gave him a trial, but I don't think he went very far with them. And during the war there was Bill Morgan. We used to call him Paddy because he was so Irish."

"I never expected to find the Irish here," Vickie said. "And I thought Morgan was a Welsh name."

"So it is, so it is. There was Adelaide Morgan I used to go out with when I was very young. She was so Welsh, hymn singing and all that. Too much even for my parents, and they were strict chapel. Adelaide didn't have much time for me on Sundays, I can tell you. You know, I think some Welsh miners were brought here in very early days when they were trying to develop some anthracite mines round here, like they have in Wales. We've got lots of foreigners here from those early days. They brought the Irish here to dig a canal down to Lincolnshire and they're still around."

An idea suddenly came into Vickie's head, something

she remembered from the social history she'd been reading. "Did you have Italians too?" she asked.

"Italians? No, we never had any Italians. What makes you think we had Italians here?"

"I had a cup of coffee this morning at the old ice-cream parlour near the town hall, and I have an idea that the Italians did all the ice-cream in those days."

"Oh, that was just one family. I forget their name. I think it was something like Mandell. Something like that. But they went away. I think they moved to Brayburn. Very nice ice-cream they made, but I didn't see much of them like family, you know. They were different. I remember they had a lot of daughters, but that's all I remember. I'm sorry I can't help you much on this programme you're doing. Will it be on television?"

Vickie left, hardly able to control her excitement at having found the name. Her hand was shaking as she finally sat down in her car, ready to switch on the engine. Not just the name: the *institution* she should have thought of, the biggest of all—the Catholic church. The Mandell daughters: their births and marriages—it would all be in the church records if she could get access and quickly. Would she have time? It was already after twelve. She was to see Volkening at the Newport Arms after 12:15, but now with a different scenario. Where was the local priest?

Ten minutes later she was in the lobby of the Station Hotel, asking the girl at the desk where she could find the Catholic church. The manager was nearby and looked at her in some surprise. Church on a Monday at twelve noon?

"Oh, if it's the priest you want, you'll have to do a little telephoning," he said, with a rather canny note in his voice at being able to present this London lady, who had arrived in the middle of the night, with a corresponding and rather intriguing puzzle at the Longbeck end.

172

"You see there are not a great many Catholics in the area, so it's all organised from Brayburn. There are some small Catholic churches in different places, we have one here in Latchmere Road, but they're only open when Father Rippel comes to take the service. He goes on to different places on different days of the week, and you'll have to telephone his home in Brayburn to see where he is. Now, he might just be here," he said, with evident pleasure at explaining the richness of the situation, "but then again he might be a long way away. I think they've even got a little church at Mortfold Green, and that's twenty miles in the opposite direction from Brayburn."

There was no point in trying to hurry him. He was going to take his time, and he took his time, in dealing with this delicate and uncertain situation. Vickie kept calm. "Have you got his home number in Brayburn?" she asked.

The number was produced and the call made. A rather sharp-voiced lady answered, his housekeeper, intent from the word go to try to impede this demanding London woman from imposing herself on Father. He was out, due back for dinner at one o'clock, but he had a long list of important engagements that would occupy the whole day, the first being at 3 P.M., and it would take an hour or more to get over from Longbeck, with the buses so slow.

With an unusually sharp burst of decision, Vickie suddenly dropped all the polite querying and turned on a voice of total authority. "I am driving over immediately," she said. "Tell Father Rippel that I will be there at two o'clock, and I need his attention for at least an hour." Hearing a faint noise of expostulation, she simply augmented the authority. "Let us not waste any more time," she said, acting out the grande dame to perfection. "Father Rippel will wait for my arrival. There are reasons which he will understand when I inform him."

"All the records are here," he said. "Of course it will take time to go through them, but with what you have told me, I will do it. I am going to cancel some of my church duties, personal visits mostly, or rather postpone them until later in the day. This is a strange story you have told me, and I have to think that only Providence could have brought the church in so centrally. I want to help."

Before leaving for Brayburn, she had driven to the Newport Arms and been directed swiftly to old Tom, sitting at a corner table with a pint in front of him. He was a wizened little man, immensely intrigued to have this lady descend on him and ready to respond very quickly to the proposal she made. "Mr. Jopping sent me," she said. "I have to talk to you on a very important matter for a programme I'm doing, but I have to go to Brayburn first. Could I see you here this evening? Say six-thirty or seven? We can have a drink and a talk. I think you'll be interested."

The barman gave her instructions for the journey to Brayburn. It took her fifty minutes. At 2 P.M. the housekeeper opened the door and showed her in, visibly impressed by now with the importance of the occasion. "May I give you a cup of coffee?" she said, almost submissively. "Father has a pot of coffee in his room and I will bring you a cup."

Father Rippel was small and round, exuding geniality in a style instantly reminiscent of one's image of Father Brown. There was an echo, too, in the way he had responded to Vickie's simple declaration that a Great Crime was afoot—capitals were clearly heard—and had to be prevented. There was no question of talking to him of some fictitious BBC programme. Instead, she got down to bedrock. There could be a crime. The church records might reveal what lay behind it and thus expose the crime before it could be committed. "Where do we start?" Father Rippel said with great directness. "The church records of all the area are stored here. It will be easier to go through them than with Protestants because we are relatively few, but it will still take a very long time."

He was soon turning the crinkly old pages. He himself had been resident in the area for only five years, but some Catholic names had emerged for him in conversation, particularly that of the family in Longbeck who had founded the ice-cream parlour in 1911. He remembered being told, he said, that the son of the founder had sold the business in the 1930s and retired to Brayburn itself, a seaside retirement that was very common. They had had a large family of daughters who went off in marriage at various times, with father and mother living on to a good old age, though sealed by a terrible tragedy. Brayburn's paramount war memory was the blitz of 1942, which had destroyed the steelworks and a large part of the town. The old couple had been killed. Their name was Mandell. Originally, he thought, it must have been something like Mandella or Mandello, and they had just let it slip into a slightly shorter version, certainly easier for the children at school. "Everyone loved them," Father Rippel said. "Whenever the old folks here tell me their blitz stories, they always mention the Italian couple, who were found in the ruins of their house clasped in each other's arms. Old Frank, they call him. I suppose it was short for Francisco."

Vickie was listening entranced. "I can't tell you how marvellous it is for me that I now have a base here for this Italian family."

He smiled. "But that's just the beginning. You want more, don't you?"

"The daughters," she said. "I know about one, Lucia or Lucy, who married a Longbeck man called Joseph

Morgan and then emigrated, ending up in Chicago. I presume he was Catholic. I heard that there were Morgan Catholics here.''

"Yes, we have some today; just a few.''

"There must be a record of their marriage, probably in the late twenties. They had six children. This Morgan family was the first link to Longbeck that showed up. But then we got a second link. A man in California called Antonio Paradiso married Maria Mandell, which sounds like the same family. They may have married out there, so that there wouldn't be anything in your records except her baptism.''

Father Rippel was continuing to turn the pages of the tightly packed files while he listened to Vickie. "It's going to take a long time, unless we come across some of the names by chance.''

"There's also another name to look for," she said, "though in a different way. Herbert Thomson, not a Catholic, chapel, in fact. But there may be a link, and it's important.''

Father Rippel nodded. He was turning the papers over, apparently casually but with an eye ready for anything, one felt. There was a silence for a few minutes. It was as if he was just getting the measure of the problem, without expecting factual data to emerge as yet. But suddenly, he broke off with a cry of exultation. "Oh my goodness. It's Providence. Just look at this.''

Vickie bent over the page. It was a list of marriages in January 1930. In the middle, one couple's name stood out: Joseph Morgan to Lucia Mandell.

Out of all those names! Of course it would have surfaced in time, but to find it so quickly. Old Francisco's daughter. Married in Longbeck. Emigrated with her husband to Canada and thence to the U.S.A. And the son Felix? Probably born, certainly brought up, in Chicago. If he had been born here before being taken across the

176

Atlantic, there would be a record, which would emerge in time. But wouldn't he have told her that he was born in Yorkshire? Except that so much of the Yorkshire background had somehow been concealed.

Father Rippel was still turning the papers over, looking for more marriages, baptisms, or burials with the names she had mentioned. As she watched him, the stuffy air of the little room became insupportable. The long drive, the pressure of the Longbeck enquiries, and then the drive to Brayburn were too much. She needed air or she would faint. "I must go out," she said. "Is the sea near this street? I simply must get some fresh air."

"That is exactly right," he said. "I shall go straight on. I know now what to look for. Do you have to be back in Longbeck at any special time? I will cancel my appointments and stay with the job. We must do it while you are here. There are things in these pages that must emerge. I don't know how, but God will help me."

Vickie had risen to go. "We really need a computer," she said, feeling a great warmth for this man's readiness to work on his own, in a stuffy little sitting-room, without benefit of the vast American apparatus. . . .

Father Rippel held up his hands in horror. "The work of the devil," he said, "turning human beings into machine fodder. That is not the way to deal with God's children: *this* is the way, in church records, each one individual and personal. And we shall get an answer from this, you will see."

It was not said pompously but happily, with a serene kind of confidence. Accompanying Vickie to the door, he called for the housekeeper. "Miss McKenzie is going out for a little while," he said, "but will be back within the hour. If you will put a kettle on, we shall have a nice cup of tea when she comes back." He saw her leave and went back to his room.

It was four o'clock before Vickie was back. The housekeeper, obviously impressed by Father's attention, greeted her politely, even warmly. Tea was brought in, with two plates of sandwiches and a large fruitcake. To begin with, Father Rippel said nothing about his researches. "You must have tea first, and then we can talk. I'm sure you need the tea, and I do, too."

The sea air had restored her; as she gobbled up the sandwiches, she realized how hungry she had been. Throughout, she had one eye on a page of notes that lay on the table by Father Rippel's side. He smiled, noting it, and was now ready.

"I've got something for you," he said. "I haven't asked you what the underlying issue is because I take you to be a serious person. I'm just here to be a kind of anonymous helper. You want to know all about the Mandell family, and if that means a full picture, I have to disappoint you. I've tried to absorb everything at speed, and as far as our records here are concerned, the family runs into the sand. To begin with there are lots of daughters, but then they go off and disappear under other names. A lot of them may have emigrated to America or Canada or Australia, as many Italians did. Once one member of the family settled over there, the others would follow. They would marry and settle down. Absolutely no way of tracking them very quickly."

"But you say you do have something for me."

"Well, I think so. I've got four marriages for you. Three of the girls married here but went off out of the records; they must have moved elsewhere. No children that I can spot. But there's one that I think is what you want. The youngest daughter, Anna, married a local man in 1935 and had two children, a boy in 1939 and a girl in 1941."

"Whom did she marry?"

"A Longbeck man called Daniel Kenny. He was Catholic, of course. It's an Irish name."

"What happened to them?"

"He died in 1942 and was buried here in Brayburn. And that's the last mention there is of the Kennys. Of course, some of the old people here might know when we ask them, but you say there's no time."

Vickie looked at her watch. "I've arranged to see an old Longbeck man this evening, at six-thirty. He may have known Kenny and can tell me what happened. If he doesn't, he may put me on to someone who does."

"Shall I go on looking here?"

Vickie hesitated. "There's so much more I want to know, and yet this may not be the way. Perhaps you know some of the factual things already. For example, I assume that the Kenny children were baptised. What were their names?"

"The boy was called Frank, like his grandfather, and the girl Margaret."

It was near enough to make Vickie gulp. Frank could easily become Felix. But the Morgan name, and the Paradiso name. What did it mean?

"One more thing," she said. "Did the name Thomson, Herbert Thomson, show up anywhere in the records you've seen?" He was shaking his head. "If it does," she went on, "when you're looking through any of these papers, would you let me know? Here's my address."

He was silent, putting the files together, and then said: "Do you think you've learnt anything useful, I mean on the central thing, the crime?"

"Yes," she said. "I think we may be able to stop it, through the truth becoming visible. I'm not a Catholic, but I have a kind of religious feeling about this. You know, I'm a historian; my mind's full of the motives that dominate history—ambition, power, revenge. But at this moment I feel that something is stronger than all that. I think that love can change things."

He took her hands in his. "God bless you," he said. She went with him to the door, and was on her way.

* * *

Tom Volkening was waiting for her. The glass on the table in front of him was almost empty. He gladly accepted another pint, and she took one too, marvellously refreshing.

"Mr. Jopping told me," she began, "that you remember everything about the old days."

His eyes twinkled. "I went in to see him this afternoon," he said. "I thought I'd better find out what it was all about. He says you're a writer, for the BBC, is it?"

There was a delightful alertness in his face and his small bony frame. One thought, inevitably, of a Yorkshire terrier, but there was great warmth there too. A man to trust, Vickie thought.

"I'm trying to look back forty years or more to make some connections," she said. "It's really important. If I can find out about some people in Longbeck at that time, it will help."

"I'll tell you everything I know," he said, raising his glass to salute her. "Well, at least what I can remember. Who are you interested in?"

"Did you know a young man at the time called Herbert Thomson?" she asked. "Is there a Thomson family you happen to know? Perhaps they had a son who was trained as an engineer. I can tell you the point of this question; it might help a memory to come back. Have you heard of Lord Cranford, chairman of a huge engineering company in London? He may have lived here as a boy? There may have been something about him in the local paper?"

"In the *Gazette,* you mean?" He shook his head. "It doesn't ring a bell at all." He laughed, taking another swig of the beer. "I'm not going to be very helpful, I think."

"Oh, yes, you are," she said. "That's just *one* of my

180

questions. I'm really much more interested in another family. I've already found out a lot that I wanted to know, but you can probably tell me more. I had coffee this morning at the old Ice-Cream Parlour near the town hall. Did you know the family that used to own it?''

"You mean old Frank Mandell? Of course I did. Their name was really Mandella, he told me once, but it just got shortened on the way. They left here in 1932, went to live in Brayburn, retired. But before that, I saw them a lot. What a lovely man! And all those beautiful daughters. I think there were nine or ten, one more beautiful than the other. Most of them very tall and dark. Of course they all got married and disappeared. And then Frank and Sylvia were killed when the steelworks were bombed in 1942. That was terrible. You know he'd been very keen on the team, big contributions to the supporters' club. Terribly sad. And of course all the family had disappeared by then.''

"You knew them when they were children, I suppose. Did you go to the weddings when the girls got married?''

"One or two, I suppose. Of course they were Catholic, so there was a bit of a gap there for me. Still, I saw them. I remember going to the Morgan wedding. Joe Morgan married Lucy, I think they called her Lucia. Beautiful girl.''

"Was there a large Morgan family?''

He was getting a bit slower in responses. Vickie realised she should go more slowly. He seemed puzzled, trying to think back to the Morgans.

"I don't really remember their family," he said finally. "I remember one thing, though. Joe and Lucy went off immediately after their wedding to settle in Canada. I think that another of the sisters had already married and settled there. I never knew what happened to them after that.''

"I suppose they may have had children in Canada. Did

Mr. Mandell ever show you pictures of the grandchildren?"

"Pictures? He was always showing me pictures. Goodness knows how many grandchildren he and Sylvia had. They were very proud of them. So many, I could never keep track of them. I think some of the girls went off before they were married, to settle with other sisters. I expect they all got married. And now they've all disappeared."

"Do you remember the youngest of the girls, Anna? She married a man called Daniel Kenny, I was told."

Volkening suddenly got more alert. "Of course. How could I forget them? I went to their wedding, must have been around 1935, I suppose. That was a sad story, wasn't it?" He seemed to assume that she must have heard of it if she already knew so much about the family. "I used to see him in his workshop. I took things along to be repaired, and he would spend a lot of time showing me what he was doing. But he was never the same after the fire. He just faded away. I don't even remember when he died. During the war sometime. Around nineteen forty-two or nineteen forty-three, I suppose."

"I didn't know about the fire," Vickie ventured.

"Oh yes," Volkening said. "I think you could say that the fire killed him. Before that, he'd been so lively, so interesting."

"Was he keen on the football team?"

"No, you could never get him to go to a match, always too busy with the workshop and all that. He was very tall and skinny, never drank much, just working, working on his inventions. I knew him long before he married Anna. I took something to his workshop to be repaired. A kind of extension entry to my attic had broken off. He came round and had a look, and suggested a new idea, very simple and ingenious, worked from a lever at the foot of the stairs. Of course that was nothing compared with what he was doing in the workshop before the fire."

Vickie held her impatience in firm control. She would have to keep the pace slow. He readily accepted another pint, and she took one herself: Bramley Bitter. Extremely good. Georgeous colour. Four-Star Extra. Tremendous kick. "The fire?" she prompted.

"Yes, poor man. He showed me the drawings he'd been doing for years, an invention he was just bringing to perfection. Had to do with turning a whole lot of hand processes in working special steels into automated processes that could be adapted to very big factories. He was a very quiet man. The last man to boast. But he did say once that there was going to be a fortune in it when he was quite satisfied with it and had got the patents. We'd become quite friendly by then, when he told me what it was all about. He made me promise to keep it all very secret. No one to know. Of course I never said anything about it to anyone, not even to my wife."

"But what happened to the inventions?"

"Well, all the drawings were burnt in the fire, weren't they? And he fell into what they called a depression. Simply faded out. He did seem to recover a bit when he met Anna and they got married. She was wonderful to him. I suppose the fire must have been quite a few years earlier; I can't remember dates: nineteen thirty-one, nineteen thirty-two, or something. I used to see them after they were married. They were all alone. His parents had moved back to Ireland, and the Mandells had retired to Brayburn. Anna did everything she could to get his spirits back. He could hardly do his ordinary repairs in the workshop; no more inventions stuff, especially with all the papers burnt to ashes. Yes, she was wonderful, was Anna. She went out to work, cleaning jobs mostly, I think. And then, when he began to feel a little better, they had two children, a boy and a girl. I was in the army myself at this time, the war, no one knew what was happening to anybody. He wasn't in the army; metal workers had to do defense work. Not that he was up to much from what I heard. He was still in this depression, and I was told later he'd died.''

"And what happened to his wife and children?''

"I have some idea that they went abroad after he died. I don't really know. It's all such a long time ago. But I must tell you, Miss, that it's very interesting for me to talk about it. Brings it all back. We had some good times before the war, especially when the team were at the top. We got to Wembley, you know. I'll never forget it. And then there was the Depression, and then the war.'' He sighed deeply, taking another copious draft of his beer.

It seemed clear that there would be nothing more to come from old Tom. She tried a routine question. "Can you think of anyone else from that time who might have worked with him and might remember some things?''

"No,'' Tom said. "Before he was married he was always on his own. Never talked to anyone. Did all the repair work himself, and then sat up all night working on his inventions. He did have a young boy there sometimes helping to put things away: that sort of thing. I can remember his name, Bert, because that's my own first name, though everyone calls me Tom. So there's no one I can think of.''

With infinite patience, Vickie sat on for a little while, her thoughts turning round in a kind of triumph. A young boy called Bert. It had to be right. Inventions. A fire, with all the paperwork burnt to ashes, or so it seemed. And after the fire, Dan Kenny in a state of depression, effectively killed.

Had the Four-Star Extra gone to her head? She didn't think so. Before leaving, she had Tom's glass recharged and invited the barman to accept the same. At the hotel, ten minutes later, she began trying to get in touch with Ambrose.

It was 7:30 in Yorkshire, 2:30 in Cambridge, Mass. The colleague who accepted the collect call told her that Ambrose had gone to Washington for the day but would definitely be back in his hotel late in the evening.

The course to take was clear. She had had a long night and a long day. Some food was called for to deal with the Four-Star Extra. A steak was produced. She retired early, leaving instructions to be called at 5 A.M. At 5 A.M. she would have caught up with sleep and Ambrose would be back: midnight in Cambridge, Mass.

Ambrose was there. With names suitably disguised, she gave him a full account of what she had discovered, clear enough to lead him instantly to the conclusions she had herself reached. If the detail was missing, the bare bones of a terrible story forced itself into recognition, with a motivation for action—fearful action—that could have become obsessive. There had to be confirmation, but who else could Bert be? Felix knew, and Margaretta too. They would be in alliance, with their dark secret. But Felix was at the centre. One day he would fill out the story for her, but only if they could save him now.

She had forseen what Ambrose would say. The only way was through direct confrontation. There was certainly nothing with which to go to the police. They had to break him out of the obsession. It was the only way.

"Are we to threaten him?" she asked.

"In a sense. When he knows what we've discovered, he could call it off. He might even bring us more closely into other issues. I've been to Washington today, and have found out some Mafia aspects of the story that we thought possible. There's something there. If one only knew where he stands on all these things, we could be more confident on bringing in the police. But in the meantime—you said 'threaten,' didn't you? It's not quite that. Just to tell him we're watching. And you're the person to do it."

"I knew you'd work up to this. Of course I will, if we agree it's right. I must tell you that I've grown very close to him and he to me, I think. It makes it harder and easier."

"You must ring him now, or say at six, your time. You know his number. Ring me again when you've spoken."

"I will."

She got up, had a bath, dressed, and sat down to some coffee that had been laid on. At six exactly, she rang Felix's home number.

He answered the first ring, as if he'd known it was coming and who it would be from. Her heart was beating rapidly.

"Oh, thank goodness," he said. "I've been after you day and night. Where have you been?"

"I've been to Longbeck," she said quietly.

There was a long silence, and then he spoke, with a most terrifying calm. "You know, then?"

"I know some things, but not the full story. Are you going to tell it to me?"

Again a silence. Then, very calmly: "It's a story of lies."

"But for a reason? A justifiable reason? What led you into it?"

Silence again, as if reaching into a far distance. "Revenge. I took it on myself. A terrible thing had been done. I laid plans for a long time. It was to happen at the festival. I could do it, but I suddenly saw that it was horrible—villainous—and I gave it up."

"When did you decide?"

"It had to do with Margaretta and me. She is my sister. I expect you know that now. I was with her two nights ago and told her it was all off. She'd never really believed in it. She'd gone along out of loyalty to me. She was very relieved."

"So nothing is going to happen at the festival?"

"Nothing."

"What made you change your plan?"

"I fell in love."

Vickie let the word stay in the air. Then she said softly, "I'm driving to London this morning. I want to see you, but not immediately. Will the bad things float away now if we give them time?"

"That's what I shall live by now. I feel cleansed, like after a fever."

"You can imagine that this is a weight off my heart. Let's leave it for a time. I'm going to the festival on Saturday. I've taken a room for the night at the hotel in Ashenham—the Wheatley, it's called. Let's meet there when the performance is over, and you can tell me everything. I've worked some things out for myself, but the central thing baffles me. You say it's been going on for a long time, like a fever. It's all over now, you say."

"All over."

"Bless you," she said, and put the receiver down.

The surrounding silence from the outside world now took over. She sat still for ten minutes, unable and unwilling to bring the world back with a phone call to Ambrose. But finally she brought herself to ring the operator and get the girl to put the call through.

"I've spoken to him," she said. "Nothing's going to happen at the festival. We can relax."

"Do you know any more about the story behind it?"

"Only that it is a story of revenge."

"Will he tell us the whole story?"

"I think he'll tell me a lot, but not what he may have had to do en route. What matters is that nothing's going to happen at the festival."

"Don't count on it too much," Ambrose said. "There's always the unexpected. I have a terrible feeling in my bones. Did he say what made him give it all up?"

"He'd decided before I rang him. Something had changed him."

"Do you know what it was?"

"I think so."

"I'll risk putting it into words," Ambrose said. "It was meeting you."

"Yes, I'm sure that's what it was. I'd be happy if you didn't still have doubts. You're supposed to have an instinct. I'll try to forget it. I'm off to London in a few minutes. We shall have to meet. A great deal to talk about. Will you be in London?"

"I'm going up to the festival on Friday, staying with Jock Richards; he has a house not far off. When are *you* going up?"

"On Saturday morning," she said. "I've taken a room for the night at the hotel in Ashenham, the Wheatley."

"If you're free, we could meet in London on Friday. Lunch."

"Lunch would be fine. And oh, Ambrose . . ."

"Yes?"

"Thank you, darling Ambrose, for helping me to live through this. I only wish I could forget your instinct. You seem to feel that something will happen just when everything seems solved. Oh well, I'm still grateful."

He grunted as usual, but was not displeased.

It had been easier to talk of letting two days pass than to live through them without knowing everything behind what had emerged. But impatient as she was, she still felt it right to have asked for an interim. Her head was full of ideas that she felt she should try to work out for herself. She wanted to get some perspective, also, through a talk with Ambrose. He would know so much more than she did about the American background to the story, guessing better than she could about other factors that would help her to understand things, perhaps even to justify them.

Ambrose rang her at home early on Friday to suggest meeting upstairs at Johnston's, where the tables were widely placed, with chance for a talk. Once seated, and with drinks and food ordered, Vickie gave him a detailed account of her explorations in the north and of ideas she'd had since then.

"I've been thinking a lot about the contrast between Felix and Margaretta," she said. "Once I knew from Volkening that they were brother and sister, I wondered if we shouldn't have been able to get an echo of it. They're both very tall and good-looking, but absolutely different in Margaretta being so dark and Felix so blond. Of course the genes work unpredictably. With an Italian mother and an Irish father, you can count on something unexpected just by itself; but I wonder if he went out of his way to accentuate his natural blondness, perhaps by rinses, so that no one should take them as siblings. Obviously Cranford had no idea about the relationship. He wouldn't have known Felix's family in Chicago, and Margaretta emerged for him from the West Coast Italian background. Everything about them seems so different, brought up so far apart, Chicago and Los Angeles. Their mother must have died when they were infants in Canada, and they were taken over by their aunts. Do you think that they became American citizens by naturalization?"

"Couldn't be that way," Ambrose said, "or the computer would have brought it out. It has instant access to all official records of naturalization going back a long time. No, they must have been just absorbed into the two families separately as infants, and picked up their official status as U.S. citizens through carelessly checked school and church records. Immigrants have always done what they could to bypass all the horribly complicated formalities. It was quite easy coming from Canada, especially for children. Today there's a huge semi-illegal immigration from Mexico, but the open Canadian border led to most of it in the past. I remember we talked about it."

"I suppose," Vickie said, "that she went to Canada after her husband died, perhaps to another sister. She was worn out and died soon after. But if so, why didn't the children just stay on?"

"I can make a guess," Ambrose said. "Maybe she didn't go to a sister but just got to some stranger instead through one of the welfare organizations. It was during the war, and there was a constant stream of immigrants with small children being taken care of there. Once she arrived, she got in touch with these two older sisters in America, married and settled by then, and they proposed the arrangement. Perhaps she'd already fallen very ill. Just picture her position. Her husband had died. Her parents had been killed in the blitz. She wanted the infants to be given a solid family background that would seem natural to them in what one might call the Italian style."

"I wonder when they were told that they'd just been grafted on to these families," Vickie said.

Ambrose hazarded another guess. "I imagine it was smoothed over to begin with, and then they might have been told when they could accept the facts. By then, they had acquired solid American and family backgrounds, but they knew that they were really brother and sister, and when they met, it would have been a tremendous bond."

"All right," Vickie said. "I'll go along with that. But what about the inner drive that was consuming them? Certainly it consumed Felix. He called it a fever. It sounds as if it might have consumed her, too, though perhaps in a different way. What a terrible heritage for them as brother and sister. The fire in their father's workshop, all his inventions destroyed, his illness and death, and then their mother's death. Felix must have felt it worst, of course. Every time he heard the story, it must have grown. He probably heard more details from the aunt who acted as his mother. One can understand how it turned into anger of a kind that then dominated his life. And at some point, perhaps through something his mother had said, he identified the source."

Ambrose nodded. "She must have mentioned Bert, who had been around and then disappeared. She had been suspicious, and he took it from there."

"He must have gone into it the way I did," Vickie said. "He got to know when he worked for Masolino about Cranford's origins, and revenge then took over. He brought Margaretta in. It's a horrible thought. If she married Cranford they could get back all the money he'd amassed. It was like the Count of Monte Cristo. They were really going to go for him."

"He wasn't one to complain," Ambrose said sardonically. "Perhaps the Baxby takeover is what happens all the time in business, but the original villainy, if he set Kenny's workshop on fire, is really deep-dyed. He would have been watching what Kenny was doing, and heard, as Volkening did, that when these inventions were patented, they would lead to a fortune. So one day he goes into the workshop late at night, takes all the important engineering papers, scatters a lot of other papers around, to yield the ashes, and sets it all ablaze. He stays in the neighbourhood for a little while after the fire, during police enquiries, and then goes off to another job and is never heard of again in Longbeck. If Fate really keeps track of things, he shouldn't get away with it, and perhaps he won't. I believe in Fate, you know."

"It's hard for me to accept," Vickie said, "because I grew to like him."

"He still hasn't talked to you about his beginnings?"

"No. But I can tell you about the psychological angle. He told me at our first meeting that he wanted a book written that would take account of his moral failures on the way up. If he began with a deliberate crime like the one we're imagining, I doubt if this was to go into the book. I began to think, after my talk in Shilton, that the moral failures that might come out were ruthless schemings in business, like the operations with Baxby that were really a form of swindle."

"And after they'd taken him in as a partner without any capital."

"I've been trying to work out how this might have happened," Vickie said. "I've constructed a picture in my mind that would lead him to the partnership. Assuming that Bert disappears with Mr. Kenny's drawings in his bag, he has to find a way, first, to acquire enough engineering know-how to be able to have the drawings presented for patenting. I suggest that he goes south, far away, to a place like the Polytechnic at Sheffield, and takes some courses at night while he works during the day on unskilled jobs in steel factories. He might give this six months or even longer, and during this time he's looking round for someone with expertise to help him to turn what he calls his own inventions into presentable form. With this experience, and with patents made out to him, he turns up finally at Shilton and is taken on at Baxby's."

"He had more than his patents, of course," Ambrose said. "He had a tremendous natural drive that was going to take him on past Baxby's and past every other firm in the way to building an international empire."

"It's still an astonishing growth, isn't it?" Vickie said.

"Do you think that the Italian connection in Chicago brought in some shady things?"

"I always wondered about that," Ambrose said. "We talked about it, you remember. I told you that I found something out on this when I went down to Washington on Tuesday. A friend of mine in the FBI told me that something might be coming out soon that would link Masolino to the Mafia. An Ohio grand jury has been working on this for some time."

"I got a hint of this from Cranford himself," Vickie said. "Talking about business methods, he said that some firms he had links with were sometimes accused of helping the Mafia to launder their money into ordinary large-scale enterprise. He said he couldn't see anything wrong in that kind of Mafia connection. It didn't worry him in the least, though of course it may worry Masolino more."

Ambrose then said, with some hesitation: "I think you might also have to be concerned about Felix Morgan's particular role in the Masolino-Mafia operations. Leaving aside his personal drive, he had to make his way in the business, and it could be that he took on some Mafia jobs for Masolino to make connections that would help him in anything—well, physical—that he planned to do about Cranford."

"Yes," Vickie said. "I've also wondered whether he established some links with the pro-Irish underground in America with the same purpose in mind. After all, he came from a solid Irish Catholic family. It wouldn't have been at all difficult for him to win their confidence."

"Plus his bomb expertise from Vietnam," Ambrose said sombrely. "With this background he could have become a totally unsuspected link for the IRA in London, getting access to arms and explosives."

"It's all too true," Vickie said. "He could have rigged the Cranford letter-bomb himself to make Cranford look like an IRA target, as a preparation for doing something real, with the same cover, at the festival. Oh, God. It could have happened, easily. The thing had dragged him in; it might have dragged him under."

"And Margaretta? Where do you put her?" Ambrose asked.

"I have to envisage a kind of mixture in her. Totally committed to her brother, and yet with a kind of sophistication that takes her elsewhere. The fact that she chose this play, based on *Les Liaisons Dangereuses*, for the festival sums it up perfectly. Cranford told me that when she gave it to him to read, he had at first just thought it very unusual and interesting, but then he'd come to hate it and won't attend the performance. If our theorising is on the right track, he's quite right to keep away. I understand it perfectly."

Vickie, leaving the restaurant, felt that the load on her mind had lightened, somehow, through the talk with Ambrose. They had confronted the likelihood of a really barbarous act years ago, followed in revenge by a villainous programme of lies and violence, but now that she had framed words for what had wandered through her mind, the evil seemed eased. Could she allow herself to believe that there might be something called a happy ending hovering somewhere, despite Ambrose's warning?

She smiled slightly, thinking of the word "happy." "Felix" meant "happy." He had been called "Frank" at birth, probably changed to Felix because there was another Frank among his new brothers. She was going to think of this as a happy omen.

10

AMBROSE, LEAVING HER, went straight down to Ashenham. The festival had started the day before, unfolding to everybody's satisfaction as culture high and low found assorted ways of expression. The organising committee of local and other notables had done their job reasonably well, with balance a major aim. The opening lecture, it is true, had not aroused universal enthusiasm: "Proust and Richardson: Some Comparisons and Contrasts" by Prof. Homer Mannering of Yale and Oxford. But it was followed by a group of Chinese acrobats who had the children open-eyed in delight. A shortened version of the old English musical "Merrie England" was just the ticket for the Suffolk evening audience, with long dresses and silken shawls much in evidence. An "Any Questions" meeting taken by three M.P.s from Suffolk was to be followed that night by the Guarneri Quartette playing Opus 135, for which every ticket was gone. On the Saturday, the cricket match was a certain winner in attention, with many sideshows available, including the famed Japanese pottery, if it rained. Tickets for the evening play, with Lady Cranford as star, had long been sold out. Lawns had been set aside for a big bowls match between the ladies of Suffolk and Norfolk. Fireworks would take over on Saturday night as finale.

The police had been given reinforced instructions to guard the house, the barn, and indeed all the grounds with intense care, and here nothing had given any cause for alarm except for what might have been an unrelated incident during the Saturday evening play. Sergeant the Hon. Anthony Brougham had been involved in an odd way, and it might have been difficult to say if it would go down in his record as a good or bad mark. Perhaps a mixture of both.

Earlier in the day he had managed to emerge with due celebrity, not as policeman but as cricketer. The two focal points of interest in the cricket match had been the prowess of Lazenby's newly arrived garage-hand as a batsman, and Ashenham's discovery at the last moment, of a sixteen-year-old demon bowler. If Ashenham had also nurtured hopes that Anthony, who had played for Oxford, would expose the weakness of Lazenby's bowlers, it was a hope destined to be disappointed. After a dazzling start with a four off the first ball, he crumbled away and was out for eleven. Ashenham had a decent score nonetheless, and the outlook seemed hopeful as Lazenby's wickets began to tumble to the demon school-boy. Only the garage-hand defied him, with sixes and fours in profusion. The score crept up. With the last man in, Lazenby were now only three runs behind. As the next ball came to Lazenby's hero, he gave it a mighty swipe that had to yield four runs and victory. The ball was whizzing at express speed past Anthony when he put up his hand at an impossible angle and caught it. Lazenby had been defeated, and all due to Anthony. He himself had no way of explaining how it had happened. He had just stretched out a hand, he said modestly, but to Ashenham he was a hero. George Sekelis called for drinks all round as they gathered in the marquee. "Class always counts, doesn't it?" he murmured to a flannelled major standing near him, with the garage-hand and the demon schoolboy well out of hearing range.

With great conscientiousness, Anthony felt that, hero or non-hero, he must now get back to his police job. Well aware of the police cars stationed at strategic points round the barn, he thought he would take a look on his own at security around the house. He took his car for the short drive and parked in a small wood east of the house. Truth to tell, he had been motivated partly by the desire to have a look at the back entrance that Billie had chosen to paint with such devotion to art. She had said that she would go back on her own the next day, and had probably done a few sketches from which she would paint a major picture later on. He had a delightful fantasy of arriving one day in Florida, perhaps to take part in an episode of *Miami Vice*, when he would see the painting, with all its memories for him, hanging on the wall in her grandmother's house. "Yes," he would say, "you've caught the scene exactly." It would be a bond between them.

She had not shown up for tea, and as far as he could tell, she hadn't attended the festival. No point in speculating what might have happened. If they met again, she would tell him.

It was a dark night under a half-moon mostly obscured by clouds. Standing absolutely still in the dark, he thought he detected a sound of slight movement and froze. Waiting silently, he heard a more explicit sound: a footstep; and there, coming toward the house, he saw a man carrying a bag and walking with a poacher's stealth. The man was dressed in what could be a poacher's leggings and a long pocketed jacket. Yet to Anthony, brought up in the country, this was no poacher. Even in the half-dark, he could see that the bag was wrong, the clothing and especially the shoes not right. He waited a moment longer, and then jumped forward.

The man dropped the bag and grappled with him. Anthony got hold of an arm and threw the man to the ground. Without a word he tightened his grip, forcing the man to his feet. "Pick up the bag," he then said, while twisting the arm with total indifference to the man's sudden gasp of pain.

The man picked up the bag, and Anthony began the march to his car. Holding the man with one arm, he reached into his pocket for his key, with the intention of getting the bag put into the boot. The man suddenly knocked Anthony over with his shoulder and twisted his arm free. Anthony grabbed at him when the man, a hulking brute, banged into Anthony and threw him forcibly to the ground. Anthony felt a piercing pain in his ankle. The man took the bag and fled into the dark. With intense pain, Anthony got the car open and radioed the police, to indicate the area in which the man might be caught. As there might be a car as getaway, Anthony aimed for the concealed entrance and drove, in agony, towards Ashenham. There was no sign of the man. At the police station he gave more details of the encounter, after which they drove him to the cottage hospital to have his ankle strapped up.

Was it a good or bad mark? He had foiled what might have been an attack on the house, but he had lost his man. One thought made him smile grimly, despite his pain. It was through Billie that he'd got into this. She had reentered his life somehow. She was unpredictable and was likely to give him trouble if he ever saw her again. But it was good to think of her.

Vickie and Ambrose were standing at the far end of the barn when the bomb went off. Before the confusion took hold, they had seen Margaretta and her opposite number, Patrick Hearn, still standing at the centre of the stage, with the applause finally dying away. There was a glimpse of Felix mounting the stage from a series of steps on one side. The scene then dissolved into chaos. Loudspeaker shouts from the police could be heard telling everyone to stay where they were, lying on the ground, until they got further instructions. There were police whistles and car gongs. A little later, there were ambulance sirens. Then there were further calls from the police telling everyone to march out very slowly through the doors and follow directions given by the police constables outside.

Vickie and Ambrose had looked at one another with a special kind of horror, not so much for their own safety as for the tragedy that had come back after all the signs of an end to the fever. "Let's go this way," Vickie said to Ambrose. "The bomb certainly came from the house. We can get to it by this path, I think."

As soon as they came out of the barn, they saw that the house was in flames. Within a minute, the flames shot up still further, as if a particularly inflammable part of the old house had now surrendered. There was a police cordon round the house, and the first ambulance arrived. Behind it they heard an old-fashioned tinkling bell signalling a fire-team, probably from the village.

Unknown to them, Felix and Margaretta had rushed out of the barn and leapt into Margaretta's car parked close to the barn. With the police cordon not yet instituted, they had dashed into the house to find Cranford, who had been sitting downstairs in his study, with a mass of papers before him now ablaze. The fire had already finished him: he was immobile. Running forward, they had just grasped his arms when a sudden burst of flame took hold and loosened the ceiling with a tremendous crash all around them. All three were knocked to the floor, with ceiling timbers around and on top of them. Their clothes were all on fire when the police and ambulance men got in. With ceiling and roof beams still falling, the rescuers could just get hold of the victims and drag them outside. A doctor leapt out of the ambulance. In a quick examination, he made it clear that Cranford and Margaretta were dead, with Felix just alive. An ambulance went off with Felix, the doctor sitting by his side. Another ambulance came up, into which Cranford and Margaretta were carried. No one moved Vickie and Ambrose away. They stood there, not knowing what to think or say.

An inspector of the Suffolk Police was standing near them, and they heard him say to the sergeant from the same force: "There will have to be an enquiry. The warning message from the IRA came in half an hour ago, but we never got it. It was one of those official IRA messages but it got stuck on the way some place or other. We could have cleared the house. It might have saved all this."

Vickie, going over to the inspector, introduced herself as a close friend of Felix Morgan and asked where she could find him now. "The Ashenham cottage hospital," he said. "I don't know what state he's in, or whether they will let you talk to him."

She raced off to her car, with Ambrose at her side. In fifteen minutes they were in the hospital and told to wait. It took an hour before a sister came out to see them.

"He's in a terrible state," she said. "Terribly burnt and with great head wounds. The doctor doesn't know . . . He says it's very bad. If you think you can take it, you can go into the room, but I don't think he can talk."

She shepherded them into a small room, where oxygen and other equipment were assembled, and two nurses standing by to do what they could. Vickie went near. He didn't seem to know her. She stood on one side and then went out with Ambrose to see if the doctor was available.

When they found him, he shook his head, but didn't try to drive them away. "Can you sit in the waiting room for a while?" he said. "When the sedation wears off a little, he may want to talk, if he can. We'll call you. Don't go away."

The waiting seemed endless, but suddenly a nurse was at their side. They followed her into his room. This time he was awake. He recognised her, and there was something like a smile in his eyes. He seemed to try to talk, but nothing came out. She put her hand on his. The smile seemed to grow stronger. Again he tried to speak, and this time a faint sound came out. She bent forward to listen. There was so much she wanted to know, not now but later, when his strength came back: the discoveries, the plan for revenge, the adventures, the misadventures—it would all have absorbed her. . . .

Not now. All he would say now, if he could speak, was a word of love. She laid her hand on his, but his eyes closed. The nurse, standing by her side, put an arm around her shoulder. His eyes opened again for a tiny smile, and then he was gone.

11

THE IRA SEEMED to have determined that there should be no doubt this time on who had decided to go for Lord Cranford. Their "warning," in recognised terms, had reached the police too late to prevent casualties; but in a proud boast later they reaffirmed that the bomb was theirs and only the first event in their new campaign on the English mainland.

No one told them, apparently, that in reaffirming their boast they were digging their own pit. A British public which might have accepted the death of one individual, growled into ferocious anger for the death in one act of three people, including the man's wife. A newspaper came out instantly with the offer of a large reward for information. Two big businesses joined in. The cash for a tip-off mounted speedily and was highly publicised.

With calls for an IRA defeat heard everywhere, the acclaim was tumultuous for Detective Inspector George Green when he was able to announce, two days later, that the villains had all been caught. Acting on information received, as he put it, a police force of one hundred and fifty, supported by helicopters, had surrounded a house in Kilburn just before dawn and picked up all those responsible, four men and a woman. The house had been found to be crammed full of arms and explosives. The capture was a decisive coup. The commissioner of police crowned Green's triumphant appearance on TV by letting it be known to the crime reporters that the inspector had been promoted to the rank of superintendent. The public breathed a sign of relief. With Detective Superintendent George Green in charge, life had become safe again.

Within the general relief, one man, Warren Faversham, was walking around in torment. The newspapers had reported that a great mass of Lord Cranford's papers had gone up in flames, but there seemed no way of knowing if this included the Masterson report, detailing Faversham's role, years before, in passing information to his Communist control. Two days after the bomb he was able to see George Sekelis for a quick word at the annual gathering of antiques dealers at Grosvenor House. Sekelis told him that the man detailed to break into Pelham Court during the play and purloin the Masterson report had been surprised by a policeman and had had to run off. If any of the papers had survived the fire they would be in the hands of trustees, and one would never know if the Masterson report would surface at some point.

For once, Sekelis was not making a joke out of things, and this matched Faversham's own view. He had to give up hoping that the fear could be banished. At any time it could come out, as had happened with Blunt. He left Sekelis and walked along Piccadilly towards the Aston office with a grim feeling in his heart. There was to be a meeting of directors and editors at four that afternoon to consider what action they should take now that they had lost their chairman. Emilia Marritt had organised the meeting, to take stock without delay. The financial director would be reporting on whether the support Cranford had provided would disappear to his trustees, to await disposition later in his will.

The directors had suggested that Emilia should chair the meeting. There was an unformulated hope that if there was a financial problem ahead, she, with her new wealth and obvious ambition, would agree the funds. She had invited editors as well as directors to the meeting to bring them all together. Not a bad move, Faversham had to concede.

All this was very normal, in these very abnormal circumstances. But the gnawing fear remained. Where was Masterson's report now? Faversham had a strong feeling that Fate always caught up with one. For no reason that he could identify, he felt that something like this had been demonstrated in the grim scene at Cranford's house on the night of the fire. The Greeks had thought this way and they were right. Fate was not to be shunned. It was a law of nature, and it lay in wait when one least expected it.

Emilia Marritt, looking round the gathering she had assembled at Aston's, was taking a pleasanter view of how Fate might choose to work. She was in Grandfather's chair in Grandfather's old room. It had always been ordained that this would happen one day, and now it had. To her audience, seated very closely around the lengthened table, she was cool and emotionless: a prim figure clothed appropriately in black. Inside, she was as taut as an E-string.

The sense of power that had taken hold of her since she gained the inheritance had moved up in successive stages. Even before Lord Cranford's death, she had come to feel that she was going to win through. With this built-in authority possessing her, she had made short shrift of the idiotic O'Leary proposals conveyed to her by Rhodine's new friend, Billie. Billie herself had to recognize that Tim was not going to get anywhere against a dame like this. And whatever strength Emilia displayed at that point came out with still greater force after Cranford's death. She knew now that she had simply to take charge. Her speech to the gathering was a perfect illustration.

"We have to consider," she said, "what steps we should take to cope with this great tragedy. Our first task will be to choose an acting chairman, until we can judge the full extent of what now faces us as a company. I won't list the problems ahead. One, very obviously, is financial. Our company is immensely strong in personal terms and in the material we own. But sometimes a position like this can be weakened by other people's moves. There was talk under our late chairman of the advisability of linking up with a much bigger group to give us financial manoeuvrability. This is a question the directors will want to discuss in due course. I rather think there would be strong objection to such a plan, especially if finance becomes available in other, more acceptable, ways. But this, in any case, is one of the pending questions hanging over us. We also have to consider urgently a number of proposals for books in new series, where the issue is both financial and personal judgement. In all these and other matters we need an acting chairman to guide our discussions, so I called in the senior editors as well as the directors. Would anyone like to make a proposal?"

It was obvious enough what would happen. Emilia by acclamation, not literally with shouts of hurrah, but with quiet satisfaction that someone so obviously capable was now in charge.

Emilia thanked them for their confidence. She would do her best to deserve it, she said. "I am going to propose," she went on, "that the meeting in this form now adjourns, with directors remaining for a directors' meeting. But before that happens, I have something in hand which I think editors should hear, too."

There was a slight stir around the table. It was hard to think what the new acting chairman might have in mind.

"I felt," Emilia said, "that we should find a way, in the shadow of this great tragedy, of saying something

206

about the chairman who came forward when we needed support and has now left us. We all had our own experiences with him at the personal level, and it might be hard to find a common expression of our sorrow. But I think there is one person from outside who can speak for us in a direct way, and I invited her to come here today. She agreed, and if this is the will of the meeting, I will ask her to join us. She is Victoria McKenzie, author of a famous life of Paul Kruger, and the special relevance of her coming here today is that our late chairman gave her a substantial contract to write his biography, to be published by Aston and Wren. She has been working on it for a little time now, using his personal archives in the first instance, and she also had a number of important personal conversations with him. The contract he gave her allowed him to refuse to publish it during his lifetime if he so wished, but she has permission to publish it in any form she likes after his death. So as you see, there is a direct Aston and Wren interest."

Vickie felt strangely moved when she came in. She had no idea as yet if she would write the book and publish it, now that she knew what she did; but in this room she was confronting a different kind of Cranford, the man who had talked to her about himself, and his desire to reach an assessment of life in moral terms. She spoke in this vein for a short while, and then said that she could give an illustration of the moral issues in life that he had expressed to her in a very unusual conversation.

"He had been given some detailed information," she said, "about a Communist who had actually been involved in espionage as firmly as all the others who have been exposed. But this man had given it all up freely many years ago, and now faced a threat of exposure. If the exposure was made, this man's life was over. So Lord Cranford tore up the documents that had come to him. In effect, without communicating with the man, he had given him his life back. I must immediately say that I have no idea who this man was, but Lord Cranford had made it his business to find out everything he had to know about the man, and decided that he had paid enough for his folly and should be left alone."

Faversham, listening, felt a wonderful peace descend on him. The fear had gone. He was free.

Even without this, Vickie seemed to have touched some deep feeling in her audience. There was a round of applause, and the meeting broke up. Would she write the life, she wondered. Probably not, she thought. She might, instead, tackle a study of social life in northern Yorkshire, back to old Tom Volkening and Bramley Four-Star Extra. Aston and Wren could publish it. In a roundabout way, this would be her real tribute to Cranford.

Anthony had recovered the use of his ankle and was in the spacious office of Superintendent George Green, who sat as usual with his feet on his desk, though at a much bigger one. Most people at the Yard knew that George had been given the accolade because it was surely his turn. He had been around. He would be retiring fairly soon. Let him retire on a superintendent's pension and good luck to him.

The news of the promotion had filtered through to his friend Zeb in the FBI who had chosen this moment to ring up from Washington to offer his congratulations. After a certain amount of badinage, Zeb turned to a practical question. They were on the red line, and could speak freely even if they wrapped up names and other details out of force of habit.

"There was a bit of unfinished business that I left with you," he said. "A character of evil disposition that we keep track of had arrived in London from Amsterdam and rang a certain lady in the advertising business—it

208

was a Friday afternoon—about a contract that was likely to be set up. Do you remember?''

"Certainly," Green said. "If there's been a new development, I'd like Sergeant Brougham to listen in. He happens to be in my office at the moment.''

Anthony, instructed by a nod, picked up the extension and listened.

"The advertising lady was told," Zeb said, "that someone would get in touch with her a few days later, on Wednesday, to get the contract moving. Your people were going to watch out for her callers and take it from there. But you reported that nothing happened. No tough guy from America showed up, so it was a dead letter.''

"Yes," Green said. "I remember all that. Is the story starting again?''

"It never stops, and never comes out nice and clean," Zeb said in an aggrieved tone. "The man we follow certainly has people everywhere and sets them up to do the actual jobs, but we don't know what any of these men look like. They must be very different from what we expect, but in what way? It's baffling.''

"I can see that," Green said. "Is he coming back to England for a new job? Of course, we'll do everything we can to help.''

"Not England," Zeb said. "He went off to Florida last week, to Miami, and we're sure he's got a contract for some of his usual work down there. Miami's our new headache now. No way of getting on top. It's a crazy world; you can't separate the cops from the robbers. Everything's upside down. And they all love it. Have you seen that programme *Miami Vice* on your TV? Just like that.''

"No, I watch *Cagney and Lacey*. What nice girls. I wish they worked at Scotland Yard. But where do we fit in with Miami?''

"I just wondered if you might have heard of any of

your own villains suddenly taking the trip over. I know there's a direct flight now from London. It might give us a lead."

"I'll certainly ask," the superintendent said.

It was "Miami" and *"Miami Vice"* that had suddenly triggered everything for Anthony. Direct flight from London. She obviously knew everybody there, on both sides of the fence. Zeb needed to find someone totally unexpected. How about Cagney or Lacey upside down? Wouldn't that fit the bill? "May I offer an idea?" Anthony said into the phone.

"Sure," Zeb said cheerfully. "You've solved the mystery?"

"Well, something worth exploring," he said. "I haven't had a chance to tell Inspector Green—Superintendent Green—yet, but it may lead somewhere. Just look up the passenger lists of the direct flights from London to Miami in the last week, and see if there's a girl called Billie, who has blue eyes and long blond hair, and a grandmother who lives in Palm Beach, Florida. If you can get your hands on her, you might enjoy it. And of course it may also prevent a little mayhem."

Superintendent Green was looking at Anthony with total amazement. At the other end of the wire, Zeb was equally astonished. "Wow!" he said to Green. "That's some detective you've got there."

Well, there it was, Anthony thought. No chance now of getting a role in *Miami Vice*. But he would see her when she got out, with large remission for good behaviour. He would be waiting at the gate, as in the movies. She would be a bit older, but just as beautiful. She would be expecting him, and would give him a big smile. "Hi," she would say.